Ever since Gaia had entered their lives, it had been nothing but *Gaia* this, *Gaia* that—*Gaia, Gaia, Gaia*. And Loki was going to end up with his precious little niece, just like he wanted, while Ella was left out in the cold. Well, what about *her*? Didn't she count for anything anymore? Hadn't she given him everything? But he didn't care. Perhaps he'd pushed her away because she wasn't pretty enough, wasn't young enough—wasn't *Gaia* enough.

No. She shook her head, gazing into her steely green eyes in the mirror. Her red hair was dazzling, and her porcelain face still beautiful—despite the wounds. She *was* young and pretty. She was a woman. And Gaia was a child. That was the difference.

Ella snorted. Loki might have cast *her* on the side of the road like an old hubcap, but she wasn't even close to being through with *him* yet. *There's only one way of getting the attention of a man with a one-track mind*, she said to herself. *To hunt down the thing he loves the most and kill it.*

Don't miss any books in this thrilling series:

FEARLESS™

Available from POCKET PULSE

FEARLESS™

KILLER

FRANCINE PASCAL

POCKET PULSE
New York London Toronto Sydney Singapore

To Brianna Adler

An *Original* Publication *of* POCKET BOOKS

 POCKET PULSE, published by
Pocket Books, a division of Simon & Schuster, Inc.
1230 Avenue of the Americas, New York, NY 10020

 Produced by 17th Street Productions,
an Alloy Online, Inc. company
33 West 17th Street
New York, NY 10011

ISBN: 0-671-03953-9

First Pocket Pulse Paperback printing September 2000

10 9 8 7 6 5 4 3 2

Fearless™ is a trademark of Francine Pascal.
POCKET PULSE and colophon are
trademarks of Simon & Schuster, Inc.

Printed in the U.S.A.

KILLER

In algebra and other heinous forms of advanced math, there's a lot of talk about logic. You know—if *A* equals *B* and *B* equals *C*, then *A* must equal *C*. Get it? That kind of thing. It's pretty obvious. I mean, you don't have to have a degree in rocket science to make these sorts of basic connections. Even somebody who hates math (like me) can grasp the old *A*-is-to-*B*-is-to-*C* bit.

So it's kind of strange that it took me so long to figure out that my father was the one who shot Ella on the street yesterday.

Okay. I guess I should back up a little. Actually, what I should do is break it down into mathematical terms. You know, show you the logic of it.

A. I saw my father

B. He was pointing a gun at Ella.

C. Ella got shot.

So obviously my father was the one who shot Ella. This should have been very clear to me from the moment it happened. But still, I just couldn't bring myself to believe it. Of course, that's because the idea of my father shooting my foster mother raises a lot of very disturbing questions—the kind of questions that are about as far from logic as you can get.

For starters, what was my father even doing there? All of a sudden he bursts out of nowhere and saves my life.

Oh, yeah, I forgot to mention a key part of this whole equation: Ella was trying to kill me. That actually sounds a lot more shocking than it really is. Legally she's my foster mother, but legality is about as far as the relationship goes. She's working for somebody (who, I don't know), she's trained in martial arts (again, this is a total surprise), and she's very unbalanced. Psychotic, in fact. (Why, I have no idea.) All I know for certain is that she hates my guts—and she has from the moment she met me.

Which brings us back to the incident on the street.

Recently the tension between Ella and me has been a little worse than usual. Maybe that's an understatement. If the previous tension could be represented by, say, a single Krispy Kreme dough-nut, the tension now can be rep-resented by a doughnut the size of Australia. There are a lot of reasons for this, most of which revolve around a certain Sam Moon, and none of which I feel like addressing at the moment.

All I know for certain is that I can no longer live with Ella. Again, it's just a matter of logic. It doesn't make much sense to live with a woman who's trying to kill me, right?

Luckily I have a way out.

My uncle Oliver is kidnapping me. Of course, "kidnapping" is also strictly a legal term—like "foster mother." I'll be a very willing victim. Because by kidnapping me,

he'll be saving my life. Which he's
already done on one occasion. It's
something he and my father have in
common—besides an uncanny resem-
blance. That's right.
Coincidentally, my uncle is another
blood relative who happened to
explode out of nowhere and save my
life. But I guess that would make
sense. He and my father are twins.
Why wouldn't they choose to behave
in the same totally inexplicable
way?

There's only one little catch.
Before I leave town with my
uncle—before I say good-bye to
this city for the rest of my life
(or at least until I turn eigh-
teen)—I have to find my father.

Yes, I realize that this
sounds stupid. I realize that it
defies logic. My life is in danger. But I don't have a choice. I
have to know why my father
tracked me down. He has to answer
for the past five years. Somebody
does, anyway, because I'm sick
and tired of being so confused.

Anyway, I keep imagining the conversation we'll have when I do
confront him. It runs over and
over again in my head, like one
of those adventure-fantasy books
where you choose your own ending.
Mostly it consists of me firing a
lot of questions at him. (No, the
gun imagery is not intentional.)

Why did he and Oliver have a
falling-out?

What happened between him and
Oliver and my mother?

Why did he abandon me?

The list goes on, and it takes
a lot of different paths, depend-
ing on how I imagine the way my
father responds. Sometimes I see
him falling on his knees, begging
for forgiveness. Sometimes I see
him turning his back on me.
Sometimes he's not there at all.

The last one is the scenario
that seems most likely. But this
fantasy conversation probably
won't even be an issue.

Especially if Ella recovers
from her gunshot wound.

She was nothing, less than nothing— a freelance assassin . . . . a *pawn*.

vapid and tacky

GAIA MOORE PUNCHED THE PHONE

number one last time. There were a few rings, just like before, then the high-pitched three-tone warning that made her want to grind her teeth right down to the roots.

Life in Under Six Minutes

"I'm sorry; the number you have dialed is no longer in service," the automated voice droned.

Gaia slammed the receiver down in its cradle. There had to be some sort of glitch in the phone system. Maybe everyone in Manhattan had decided to order a pizza all at the same time. Because there was no way her uncle Oliver would change his phone number without telling her. Why would he? Didn't he promise to take her away to Europe? Didn't he say that he was going to save her from her miserable existence? This was just some sort of mix-up....

She knew Uncle Oliver would eventually make good on his promises. She *knew* it. But she wasn't about to just hang around George and Ella's brownstone, waiting for him to get in touch with her. She would be a proverbial sitting duck.

Ella might not be that hurt. Of course, the last time Gaia had seen her, Ella was lying on the pavement in the middle of the park, bleeding. It was hard to tell how serious the wound was, but if Ella was as strong as Gaia was beginning to suspect, there was a fairly good possibility the stepmonster might soon return. To finish Gaia off for good.

My foster mother wants me dead.

Even now, the words in Gaia's head made little sense. It was all still too much for her to take in. Sure, they had always hated each other . . . but to go so far as to pull out a gun? If she functioned like a normal human being, Gaia imagined that she would have sweaty palms right now. Wobbly knees. She'd be quivering—like an old newspaper over a subway grate. Or like a bowl of that nauseating Village School cafeteria Jell-O. Like a normal person. She'd exhibit the signs . . . the signs of fear. Maybe she'd even hyperventilate.

But instead, as always, her mind was sharp and clear. Her movements were quick and decisive—like an animal's. She darted up the stairs to the fourth floor, her lungs rising and falling in perfect rhythm. In situations like these, there *were* advantages to being a freak of nature. She knew she had to leave. Immediately.

Gaia tore furiously through the dirty laundry scattered around her sparse bedroom, stuffing only the most essential pieces into her beat-up messenger bag.

Cargo pants—in. T-shirts and trashed sneakers—in. Black hooded sweatshirt—definitely in.

Unworn Gap capris purchased in a moment of consumer weakness—hopelessly out.

What had ever possessed her to buy a pair of pants that emphasized her grotesque calves?

One wool cap, one bottle of Cockroach nail polish. If five years of being shuffled from one foster home to another had taught Gaia anything, it was how to pack up her life in under six minutes. The secret was always keeping your personal possessions down to a bare minimum and never owning anything you couldn't ditch at a moment's notice. That went for people, too. Not that there were very many people she was leaving behind.

Gaia had never been very successful at collecting friends. Unlike Heather Gannis, who was constantly swarmed with her own ego-bloating posse, Gaia could count the number of friends she had on one hand and still have enough fingers left over to go bowling. Actually, she could count the number of friends she had on her thumb.

The only person she had left was Ed.

Ed Fargo. Shred. The good guy. Ed understood what it was like to be an outsider—a freak like her, in his own way. Ed's wheelchair was to Gaia's fearlessness as . . . what? A sickness was to a disease? A boat was to a ship? Maybe not, but he had been loyal and understanding, especially during the times when Gaia knew she wasn't so easy to understand. It crushed her to imagine a life with him. But it beat sticking around and getting killed.

Of course . . . there *was* Sam.

Sam wasn't a real friend, though. Hardly. He was an enemy. He was an insect, fit to be squashed. The lowest form of vermin on the planet. But maybe Gaia should count him, anyway, because having just one friend on the entire planet was way too depressing for words. It was hard to know exactly what Sam was to her—the ultimate crush, a failed romantic possibility, the only person she had ever loved. Most important, Sam was the betrayer of her dreams. While she had been loving him from a distance, he had slept with Ella.

Even the thought of it stung like a slap. It hurt. Physically. Even if Ella hadn't tried to kill her, *that* was reason enough to get the hell out of town.

At four and a half minutes Gaia snapped the bag closed and slung it over her shoulder. A new record. Flying down the staircase at the speed of light, Gaia's tangled yellow hair brushed the expensively framed trash that Ella liked to refer to as her "work"—trite black-and-white photos of wide-eyed kittens, open-toed shoes, and the Flatiron Building. Vapid and tacky. But that pretty much summed up Ella in a nutshell.

"Psychoslut" summed her up pretty well, too, though.

If Ella's aim with a gun was as lousy as it was with a camera, staying healthy wasn't going to be a problem. But Gaia knew now that she couldn't take that risk. Ella's entire existence was an act. Ella was trained in several martial arts—just like Gaia. Oh, yes. After that combat in the front hall about a week ago, Gaia knew that Ella was one of the few people on earth who could kick her ass. So there was no reason to assume that Ella wasn't trained to be an expert marksman, either. This whole spandex, big-hair, trophy-wife thing that Ella played to the hilt was a cover.

The question still remained, however: What exactly was she covering up?

At the second-floor landing Gaia's feet came to an involuntary halt. As hard as she tried to look away, her eyes came to rest on the very last photograph. It wasn't one of Ella's travesties—but a snapshot that George had taken of Gaia with her mother and father five years ago. Before her world had fallen apart.

Father.

Those two single syllables fired like cannon shots through her mind. It *had* been him on the street, hadn't it? The one who had shot Ella? So why had he vanished? Why hadn't he come running to save her? Why had he ditched her . . . again?

12

But his photo couldn't answer those questions. The sight of the clueless twelve-year-old girl with skinny arms and dirty friendship bracelets set in motion an endless chain of self-pity and burning anger. Gaia had been so trusting. She had actually been naive enough to believe her father would be there for her . . . forever.

Gaia ripped the photo off the wall with such raw force that a three-inch chunk of plaster came off with it. She shoved it in the bag.

Whatever. She wouldn't try to guess at her father's motives. Her uncle was there for her now. That was all that mattered.

Go . . . go . . .

Racing down the hall and into George's office, Gaia was seized with a raw, gnawing guilt. The desktop was bare except for a computer, the way George always left it when he was out of town. She wouldn't be able to say good-bye. Despite his grotesque taste in wives, George was a good man. He had been a friend of her father's. . . .

Stop thinking of—

From downstairs came the heavy *whoosh* of the front door opening.

Gaia's stomach soured at the familiar, nauseating *clack* of stiletto heels pounding on marble.

Ella *hadn't* been that hurt. No. She had clawed her way home.

13

"IT WAS A RARE MISCALCULATION,"

Failed Experiment

Pearl said, crossing her legs elegantly. "There was little I could do without seeming suspicious."

Loki's cold blue eyes scanned the impeccable appointments of Pearl's Park Avenue co-op, the apartment she inhabited whenever she came to New York. Everything reeked of money—the priceless oil paintings, the lacquered oak table, the three-quarter view of Central Park . . . and most especially, Pearl herself. From her blond French twist to her Prada shoes, Pearl had flawlessly assumed the life of an Upper East Side socialite.

So it was that much more surprising to him that she could also be so horrendously unprofessional.

"I should have hired someone more competent," Loki finally stated, his voice empty.

Pearl's manicured fingers absently brushed her Chanel suit. "You know these things don't always go as planned. They can take time."

Loki's jaw hardened. "I don't have the luxury of time," he said.

There was a silent pause as Pearl refreshed her teacup. "Loki, I'm not trying to second-guess your motives, but are you sure that's what you want?" she asked. The flatness of her tone matched his. "You've been grooming Ella from a tender age in matters both professional . . . and otherwise."

For a moment Loki glared at her, half tempted to lunge at her and crack her neck in half. Who was *she* to question what he wanted? To act with such insubordination. She was nothing, less than nothing—a freelance assassin . . . a *pawn. In his game.* But he was too tired—to attack or to deny her assertions, to do *anything.* The exhaustion ate at him like a virus.

"It's been a less than successful experiment," Loki finally grumbled. "Ella's turned from a brilliant operative into an embarrassing joke. She's consistently defied me. I won't tolerate disobedience."

Pearl shrugged. "I understand that. But she seems, well, rather harmless."

Harmless. Anger rose inside him again. "Ella almost killed my niece, right after you botched your mission," he snapped. He shook his head as he thought about how close it had been. Much too close. *Close enough for him to realize how precious Gaia was to him.* Because Gaia was more than just a lure he could use to draw his brother out from hiding whenever he needed to . . . far more. She was also the only lasting legacy of her mother, Katia. His one true love.

Sweet Katia.

A shudder passed through his bones. Katia should have been his wife. Gaia should have been his child. Tom should never have been in the picture. And even though Katia was gone now, pieces of her still remained in Gaia. So Loki vowed to keep his niece—his daughter, really—close to him forever . . . to look into her beautiful blue eyes and see a glimmer of his beloved Katia. And far more.

"Gaia is the most important person in my life," he found himself saying, almost to himself. "Are you aware of the implications her death could have had for you?"

The slender choker encircling Pearl's slender throat bobbed as she swallowed hard. "Give me another chance. I've gotten very close to Ella. No one would have an easier time neutralizing her than me."

Loki's stare remained steely, focused. Normally he didn't believe in more than one chance. But time was far too short. He didn't have time to call in another hit. Besides, Pearl's otherwise spotless record redeemed her—for the time being.

"I'm sending an e-mail to Ella, which she'll think is from her little flirtation, Sam Moon," he announced. "She'll think he's arranging to meet her at La Focaccia at one o'clock. Then I'll send one to Sam, which he'll think is from Gaia. They'll meet, and the confusion should give you enough time to slip in there and get the job done." His gaze hardened. "I want the situation taken care of by ten past."

Pearl nodded, meeting his eyes unflinchingly. "It'll be done this time," she said.

"It'd better," Loki warned. "Because if anything happens to Gaia, you'll be held personally responsible."

From: gaia13@alloymail.com
To: smoon@alloymail.com
Time: 11:42 A.M.
Re: Lunch

Sam,

   Meet me at La Focaccia at 1:00 P.M. We need to talk.

—Gaia

From: smoon@alloymail.com
To: eniven@alloymail.com
Time: 11:43 A.M.
Re: Lunch

Ella,

    Meet me at La Focaccia at 1:00 P.M. We need to talk about our future together.

—Sam

For a while I was hooked on those stupid reunion shows you see on TV. You know, the ones where some lame girl goes on *Jerry Springer* and carries on about how she hasn't seen her second cousin Bertha in *x* number of years because even though they only live a half an hour away from each other, neither one of them has enough cash for bus fare. First there's a lot of whining and tears and then *surprise!* Cousin Bertha walks across the stage and the loved ones are reunited while the audience disintegrates into a sloppy mess. I know it's total cheese, but what can I say? I seriously lived for that stuff.

I loved it because I used to imagine that *I* could be the one on TV, seeing my dad again for the first time in five years. This is how I thought our reunion would go: I'd be standing there with half a box of Kleenex wadded up in my fist while my father walks across the stage to give me a huge bouquet of yellow roses. We'd hug and cry, then cry and hug some more. He'd tell me how sorry he was for dropping off the planet the night my mother was murdered and how he never stopped loving me all the years we were apart.

Every one of his excuses for missing my birthday, never picking up the phone, and forcing me to live with foster freaks would make complete, undeniable sense. I'd have no choice but to forgive him, and the audience would turn into a bunch of blubbering idiots. And when it was all over, he'd vow never to leave me again.

Of course, nothing in life goes the way you want it to—especially not in *my* life.

So the reunion with my father finally *did* happen—and it didn't resemble anything I'd seen on TV.

Not unless you count *Creature Feature*.

A sticky
crimson stream
of blood
flowed down
her fingers.
It dribbled **little**
into a red
puddle around **joke**
her beat-up
sneakers.

a

"DAMN YOU, GAIA!"

Ella yanked off the pointy, four-inch-high instruments of torture that had made her feet throb for the last five years and pitched them out the gaping window

Blond Train Wreck

of Gaia's empty room. If the brat was still working her way down the drainpipe, with any luck she'd get a spiked heel through the skull. It was an image that nearly brought a smile to Ella's battered face.

And to think she almost had her.

The range had been short, the gun perfectly aimed. But then someone else hiding in the trees shot at Ella before she could pull the trigger. Ella hadn't been able to see the gunman but figured it was some street vigilante . . . or maybe even a friend of Gaia's. Regardless of who it was, though, the bullet had only grazed Ella's left shoulder blade—knocking her off her feet and causing her to lose a bit of blood—but it was enough of a hit to let Gaia escape.

Fortunately, Ella had been able to avoid any trip to the hospital. She knew enough first aid to handle the wound herself. Hospitals meant police, which meant questioning, which meant that Loki would find out . . . which meant certain death.

Ella padded to the bathroom and peeled off her bloodied blouse. The wound was shallow. Just a scratch, really—but a scratch that burned like fire as she cleaned it and dressed it with bandages. Gaia was most likely on her way to Loki's. They'd probably be on the Concorde before noon. Ella bared her teeth at the mirror like a rabid dog.

At that moment she hated Loki with all her strength.

Ever since Gaia had entered their lives, it had been nothing but *Gaia* this, *Gaia* that—*Gaia, Gaia, Gaia*. And Loki was going to end up with his precious little niece, just like he wanted, while Ella was left out in the cold. Well, what about *her*? Didn't she count for anything anymore? Hadn't she given him everything? But he didn't care. Perhaps he'd pushed her away because she wasn't pretty enough, wasn't young enough—wasn't *Gaia* enough.

No. She shook her head, gazing into her steely green eyes in the mirror. Her red hair was dazzling, and her porcelain face still beautiful—despite the wounds. She *was* young and pretty. She was a woman. And Gaia was a child. That was the difference.

Ella snorted. Loki might have cast *her* on the side of the road like an old hubcap, but she wasn't even close to being through with *him* yet. *There's only one way of getting the attention of a man with a one-track mind,* she said to herself. *To hunt down the thing he loves the most and kill it.*

As she searched through her walk-in closet for a clean shirt, Ella was amazed by the piles of sequins, glitter, and gold lamé she'd managed to accumulate over the years. All the glitz, all the shopping—all of it had been part of the character she'd played so thoroughly as George's wife. She deserved a rich reward for her performance . . . a *very* rich reward. Funny. Loki had promised she would have to be married to George for only a few months. Somehow the months had turned into years. Yet Loki still kept hinting that the two of them would be together and that all would be right with the world again and . . . blah, blah, blah. Another in an endless string of his self-serving promises.

It had been so long since Ella was herself that she couldn't even remember what she used to wear, what things she used to like. She grabbed a white T-shirt from George's shelf. It was the closest thing to normal clothing she'd worn since this whole charade began.

But once the blond train wreck was out of her life, things were bound to improve. When George returned, Ella would be sure to spin the story just right so that he would blame her for Gaia's running away. Maybe he'd even want a divorce. That would be a bonus.

And of course there was Sam Moon. The real prize.

Sam Moon would turn her life around. He was the gorgeous light at the end of a garbage-filled tunnel . . . and he didn't even know it. Ella found herself smiling through her pain as she continued to tend to her torn flesh. Sure, he had fallen for Gaia—hard. He was going to be devastated by her loss. He'd ignored Ella, too, just like Loki. But with Gaia gone, he'd have nobody to turn to but Ella. He wouldn't have a choice.

Ella taped the last bandage over her arm, then hurried to George's office and sank into his soft leather chair. Time to check her e-mail. The computer flickered as she turned it on, then she clicked the mouse over the mail icon. Five messages. Aside from the usual get-rich-quick Spam, there was a note from George. Ella stifled a yawn. Something about how much he loved and missed her. Poor guy. Even now, she still managed to feel almost sorry for him. Almost.

Delete.

That's when her eye caught a name at the bottom of the list.

Sam Moon.

Ella smiled. It looked like the young man had come to his senses ahead of schedule.

ED FARGO CLOSED HIS EYES AND

leaned in for another kiss.

Wow.

The fingers that had been gently raking through his hair suddenly stopped moving, and the soft lips pulled away. "Did you say something, Ed?"

Tightening his arms around Heather Gannis's waist, Ed's foggy gaze languidly trailed from

The New, Broken-Down Ed

her amber-streaked blue eyes, to the freckled bridge of her nose . . . down at last to a contented stop on the smooth legs that were draped across the arm of his chair. How did he get so lucky to be here at this point in time in the history of humanity?

"I think I said *wow*," he muttered.

Heather reached up and gently lifted his head by his chin, redirecting his stare back to her face. "What's the sudden *wow?*" she asked with a smirk.

Ed shrugged. He found himself smirking as well. The *wow* was hardly sudden. *Wow* had been screaming in his head ever since Heather had unexpectedly pulled him away from his sister's engagement party at the Plaza Hotel and into a storage room. *Wow* was every time he looked at her . . . and every time he saw the way she looked back at him. The sparkle in her eyes was exactly how he remembered it—before the accident. Every time he thought of it, *wow* smacked him right across the face.

Of course, so did doubt and insecurity. But what fun was being the guy in the wheelchair if you didn't have doubt and insecurity?

He bit his lip. It was easy for Heather to overlook his problems now. The relationship was brand-new again. Exciting. Like when they had first started going out. But in a few weeks or months she was going start to notice the hassles of the chair. Like the fact that she was in constant danger of having her toes run over. Or that he couldn't reach the box of Cap'n Crunch on the top shelf at the supermarket.

Then there was also the problem that Heather was bound to make a few comparisons between the old, working model of Ed and the new, broken-down one. The accident had changed him a lot—and not just because he couldn't walk anymore. What if she suddenly realized she was still in love with the old Ed and not the new one?

". . . What's wrong?" Heather was asking.

He jerked slightly and blinked. He was seriously spacing out. What was his problem? Why was he so worried? Heather was *here*. Now. Everything was cool.

"Uh . . . nothing," he mumbled.

She looked him in the eye. Her face was only

inches from his own. "You're a lousy liar, Fargo," she said wryly. "I've told you that before."

He swallowed. That was the great thing about Heather: She could always see through his bullshit. "Well, this is going to sound kind of weird," he finally managed. "See, after the accident I got this strange idea in my head that just because my legs didn't work, my lips wouldn't, either. Or that I'd forget how to make them work." He forced a little laugh. "I guess I had nothing to worry about."

Heather grinned. "You can't forget how to kiss, stupid. It's like riding a bicycle."

Ed raised his eyebrows. "Bad analogy for a guy in a wheelchair," he joked.

"Oops." Heather lowered her eyes. "I think you're doing great, though," she added quickly. "I'd say maybe you're even better than *before* the accident."

A smile spread across Ed's face.

Talking about Ed-and-Heather, part I, had finally begun to lose its sting. He was starting to realize that there was no point in clinging to the resentment he'd felt toward Heather for breaking up with him after he was paralyzed. What mattered was where they were headed. Ed-and-Heather, part II, had the potential to be much better, much deeper.

Heather abruptly stood and smoothed her

rumpled sweater. "I've gotta go," she announced. "Phoebe's being discharged from the hospital today."

Ed blinked. He still wasn't sure how to react when Heather mentioned her anorexic sister. He figured the best thing to do was just . . . well, just to be there. "Hey, that's good news," he said.

"I guess," she muttered ruefully. She glanced around Ed's room, making sure she had all her belongings. "I mean, it's good that she finally has enough strength to walk. But she still looks like a skeleton. And I don't know if she wants to eat. I mean, you saw her. They've been feeding her through tubes. . . ." Heather's voice trailed off.

"I'm sure your mom and dad will be right on top of it this time," Ed piped up, in what he hoped was a reassuring voice. "They won't let anything happen to her."

Heather's face darkened. "There's not a lot they can do. They can't be with her twenty-four hours a day, forcing food down her throat, then making sure she doesn't puke it up again." Her voice took on a hard edge. "Phoebe isn't going to get better unless she wants to. And right now, I don't think she does."

Ed just stared at her. *Say something funny, you moron,* he told himself. He always prided himself on the ability to bring a little levity into a dark situation. To take something miserable and whip it back into shape with a little joke. But for some reason, he couldn't think of a damn thing to say. It was impossible to make a joke out of Phoebe's condition—

Bzzzzt.

The front door buzzer rang.

Perfect timing. Ed breathed a secret sigh of relief.

Heather frowned. "Who's that?"

"I bet it's my sister," he muttered, spinning around and rolling himself through his bedroom door. "She left her keys here again. She's become a complete ditz since she got engaged."

The buzzer rang again—more insistently.

Ed scowled as he hurried down the hall toward the front door of the apartment. "Coming, Bridezilla," he mumbled.

He rolled up to the front hall intercom and pressed the talk button.

"Who is it?" he asked.

"Gaia."

Shit. Ed's heart stopped. Time was an eighteen-wheeler that had just come screeching to a halt. Gaia. Here. With Heather. Not good . . .

"Ed?"

Why do you always pick the worst times to show up? he wondered angrily.

"Ed, are you there?" she asked.

32

"Uh . . . yeah," he answered. "What's up?"

"Look, I know this is going to sound really weird, but can I hang out with you for a while? Just until I get in touch—"

"I'll come down," he interrupted. He didn't want to risk allowing Gaia and Heather to see each other. True, the tension between them had subsided a little. . . . But still, he knew how combustible they could be. Like gas and fire.

He threw open the front door and slammed it behind him—hurrying out into the hallway toward the elevators. He punched the down button. He rubbed his hands on his jeans. His palms were moist. So Gaia wanted to hang out for a little while. Why? And why couldn't she have called first? But there was no point in trying to make any sense out of Gaia. Besides, it wouldn't have made a damn bit of difference if she *had* called. He still would have let her come over. The pathetic truth of the matter was that he'd still do anything she wanted. . . .

The elevator doors slid open.

Ed's face twisted in a scowl as he rolled in and jabbed at the button for the lobby. He would just tell her no. Plain and simple. She couldn't walk all over him. Well . . . okay, she *did* sound a little freaked out. He swallowed. Okay, maybe he'd find out what her deal was, and then he'd decide whether or not she could come in. That was fair. She owed him an explanation. She wouldn't be able to give him the runaround. Not this time. They'd long since agreed to scrap their no-questions policy.

The doors slid open again. Ed hurried out and headed across the lobby to the glass doors.

He nearly fell out of his chair.

What the hell?

This was bad. Very bad. Gaia was standing there . . . only for once in her life, she didn't look heart-stoppingly gorgeous. Sure, she still towered over him like some modern-day Amazonian goddess, with her tangled yellow hair tumbling in a sultry mess from beneath a wool cap—but her skin was frighteningly pale. Hanging off her muscular shoulder was a messenger bag, crammed to maximum capacity, with a wrinkled shirtsleeve poking out of the top. Her left wrist was cradled in her right hand. A sticky crimson stream of blood flowed down her fingers. It dribbled into a red puddle around her beat-up sneakers.

Ed couldn't speak. He could only gape at her as he opened the doors of his building.

"Is it cool if I come in?" Gaia asked in a stony voice, seemingly oblivious to her injuries.

In an instant Ed forgot all about the promises he'd just made to himself. Gaia was hurt. Gaia needed help.

That was all that mattered. "Uh . . . yeah—sure," he stammered. "What's going on?"

Gaia brushed past him and marched toward the elevators, her head down. "I don't feel like talking about it," she said.

That figured. Of course. Why would she ever feel like talking about it? Anger surged through him, then quickly subsided. He sighed. She played the same freaking scenario over and over again: Shut Ed out as much as possible, then come to him only when you need something. Lather. Rinse. Repeat . . .

"I don't know why you're coming to me," Ed stated, following in her footsteps like some kind of sniveling puppy on wheels.

Gaia wiped her nose on her sleeve, avoiding his eyes. "I don't have anywhere else to go, all right? Don't worry—I'll stay out of your hair. All I need is a floor to crash on." Little droplets of blood marked her trail across the lobby. He glanced nervously behind him, just to make sure nobody could see.

Ed wanted to stay firm, to stand up for himself, but it was too late. She was already entering the elevator. He had no choice but to follow. He nodded at her wrist as the doors slid shut behind them. "Let me guess—a band of nomadic ninjas jumped you on the number-nine train."

Gaia looked down absently, as if she didn't have a

clue what he was talking about. "Oh. Right. I got caught on the rain gutter on the way down from my room."

"Oh," Ed said, nodding. "Of course. The old escape-from-Alcatraz trick. Got it."

But Gaia didn't seem to catch the sarcasm in his voice. Man. This was even worse than it looked. She was seriously out of it.

The elevator lurched to a stop. The doors opened. They had reached Ed's floor. Maybe it was time to drop the bomb.

Ed hesitated in the hall as Gaia walked to his door.

"So are you going to let me in?" she asked, glancing back over her shoulder. Another drop of blood splattered on the floor.

"Uh . . . yeah," he murmured. "There's something I should tell you, though."

She sighed. "What's that?"

He rolled up beside her and put his hand on the doorknob. For a moment his gaze skittered across Gaia's perfect features. He couldn't help but wonder what her reaction would be. Disappointment? Or— hope against hope—maybe even a little bit of jealousy?

"Well?" she demanded.

Ed pushed open the door, bracing himself for the storm that was about to erupt. "Heather's here," he said.

GAIA SUDDENLY FOUND HERSELF

The Burning

wishing Ella's bullet hadn't missed its mark. Even death seemed like a better alternative than being holed up in Ed's tiny East Village apartment with *her*.

Ed slammed the door shut behind them. Gaia found herself staring straight into Miss Heather Gannis's genetically perfect features: those amber-flecked eyes, that long brown hair. This was perfect. Just perfect.

Silence enveloped the room. It seemed to fill every corner, like a poisonous fog—suffocating them. Gaia continued to meet Heather's steely gaze. Neither of them blinked. Neither looked away. Gaia had to hand it to the girl: For all her bitchiness and self-absorption, Heather Gannis was tough. No wonder boys flocked to her.

"That's not your sister," Heather finally stated.

Gaia frowned. What the hell was that supposed to mean? She turned on her heels. Enough was enough. Clearly she was raining on a parade she wanted no part of. "You know what?" she muttered. "I think a park bench will be just fine." She reached for the door.

"Wait a second." Ed blocked her way, tugging at the sleeve of her battered army coat. "You can't go. You're bleeding. . . . We've got some bandages."

37

She rolled her eyes. "Ed, I'll be fine—"

"Shut up, Gaia," he snapped.

Whoa. She almost flinched. She froze, her eyes narrowing. Ed actually looked pissed. Then again, she supposed he had a *right* to be pissed. She'd barged in on him without warning, bleeding all over his apartment building—and now she was stomping away. Maybe she should just keep her mouth shut. Maybe she should just let him take care of her. It was the least she could do. Her gaze flashed to Heather.

Heather's eyes turned to ice. She sniffed, shook her head, then stormed into the living room.

"Come on," Ed mumbled.

Wordlessly Gaia allowed him to lead her into the bathroom. He turned on the faucet, then began rifling through the cabinets. She couldn't help but notice how jittery he was, as if he'd just downed a double espresso. He kept running his hands through his hair, opening the same doors over and over again.

But could she blame him? She'd be jittery, too—if she were in his shoes.

No, you wouldn't, she reminded herself. Of course not. Gaia Moore didn't *have* jitters. She was a freak. And that was probably a good part of the reason Ed's once-and-future girlfriend, the heinous Heather Gannis, hated her so much. Well, that and the fact that Gaia had nearly gotten her killed.

But there wasn't much point in feeling sorry for herself right now, was there?

Finally Ed found what he was looking for: rubbing alcohol and gauze.

"So what happened to you, anyway, Gaia?" Heather's sour voice drifted down the hall. "Did you get run over on your way to the Salvation Army?"

Ed's head whipped around. His eyes were blazing. The dark blue vein at his temple looked like it was about to burst. "Can you two do me a favor?" he asked loudly. "Can you just be quiet—"

"You don't have to worry, Ed," Heather interrupted. "I'm going to see Phoebe, remember? So you two can have a lovely time here by yourselves." Her voice oozed with venom. "How does that sound?"

Gaia winced. "He didn't want to let me in," she found herself saying. There was something insanely perverse about trying to smooth things over between Ed and Heather, but the sight of Ed's tortured face tore at her conscience. "He owes me a favor. It's time to pay up."

"Whatever," Heather called back. The front door slammed so hard that the entire apartment seemed to rattle.

Ed shook his head. His jaw was clenched. His lips twitched. Gaia swallowed. She wanted to apologize. . . .

But despite her guilt, she couldn't help feeling annoyed. She just didn't get it. First Sam went berserk over Heather and now Ed. What was it about that hideous creature that made smart, attractive guys completely lose their minds? Did an unhealthy obsession with fashion trigger some override switch in guys' heads? Was it a mindless devotion to the latest trends that kept them from noticing when a girl was a spoiled, self-absorbed snot?

"Hold still," Ed instructed, grabbing the bottle of alcohol. He tore off the cap in quick, jerky motions. "This might sting."

Was it Gaia's imagination, or did something in Ed's voice hint that he *wanted* it to sting? She held out her arm, bracing herself for the shock of pain. Maybe now would be a good time to see if Ed was planning on kicking her out when he was done tending to her.

"Where should I put my stuff?" Gaia asked tentatively.

"The spare room would be all right," he muttered, seizing her wrist.

He didn't look up. He simply splashed the clear liquid from the bottle onto her open wound.

But somehow the burning wasn't all that bad.

As far as I've figured out, there's two kinds of people in this world:

A. Those who know what they want and go after it;

B. Those who muck it up for the rest of us.

Care to guess which one Gaia Moore is?

She's probably talking trash to Ed right now, trying to change his mind about me. It would almost be funny if it weren't so unbelievably pathetic. Does she really believe I can't see what's going on here?

Anyway, I thought she wanted Sam. Fine. If she wants him now, she can have him. I'll let her win this time. She can twist Sam's mind in whatever way she wants.

But Ed—he's not negotiable.

The way Gaia's acting is hardly a surprise. She's always wanted whatever I have. But the way Ed's acting is really pissing me off. Doesn't our past together mean

anything? Ed and I have *history*.
Ed and Gaia have . . . what? Five
months? Nothing. Zilch. Nada.

Yet for some reason he keeps
coming back for more. She's got
him on some kind of short leash.
And he doesn't even see it.

Whatever. I've got enough to
deal with. I really don't need
this crap right now.

You want to know what sucks?
Being in a wheelchair sucks.
Having a girlfriend who is pissed
at you sucks. So does having a
drunken sister who plans on marrying a guy named Blane. So does
the fact that Blane's IQ rivals
his shoe size.

But I digress.

What really sucks is this:
having two people—people you
really care about—hate each
other.

Yup. That has to be one of the
worst feelings in the world.
Right up there with listening to
Barry Manilow. It's torture. See,
since you care about both of
them, you can understand why they
each feel the way they do. And
also know why they're both wrong.
So you're sort of hanging like a
battered bridge between the two
of them, over this raging river,
hoping it doesn't sweep you away
and wishing they could see each
other the way you see them.

Both sides think you're nuts,

of course. They just see that
you're hanging out there alone,
looking like an ass.

If I really wanted to, I could
sit Heather down and try to convince her that Gaia isn't as evil
as she thinks. Or I could tell
Gaia about what a great person
Heather really is. But there's no
point to it. They've already made
up their minds about each other.
And both are too stubborn to
admit that they might be wrong.

So the battle continues, with me
hanging out there in the middle—
looking like an ass.

. . . Well,
one thing was
very clear.
Her foster
mother was a
woman **secrets**
who took
immense
pleasure in
inflicting
maximum pain.

ED PUSHED A CARDBOARD BOX MARKED

Heather Defined

Christmas Ornaments under the computer desk to make room on the floor of the spare room.

"You can put your bag over here for now," he said. "I'll get some blankets and towels out of the closet before you go to bed."

"Thanks," Gaia mumbled.

For a moment he waited for Gaia to say something more—*anything*—to make him feel like he was a friend and not some chump she just used and tossed away like yesterday's *Daily News*. He wasn't asking for much. Just a little small talk. *Did you hear we're supposed to get snow tonight? I could really go for a doughnut right now.* Anything. He didn't even need to hear why she had suddenly decided to run away from home at this particular moment or why she was in such a daze. That could come later.

"Do you want something to eat?" he asked, mostly to fill the painful silence.

She shook her head. "Nah, I'm good."

"How about a Coke?"

"No, thanks," Gaia answered. "I'd like to check my e-mail, though."

Ed nodded at the computer, happy there was finally *something* he could provide for her. "It's yours, anytime you want."

46

Without saying a word, Ed watched Gaia plop down unceremoniously at the desk. She tucked a snarled strand of hair behind her ear and stared at the screen in concentrated silence. Ed shook his head. Already his presence seemed to have been forgotten. Gaia might be going through some kind of crisis, but she didn't have to be *rude*. He turned to the door. Although he could maneuver his wheelchair throughout the apartment with the precision of an Olympic skier competing in the giant slalom, Ed deliberately ran into the doorway as he backed out. Okay, yes, it was a cheap stunt to get attention. He knew it. But it was worth a shot. He felt like he was about to burst.

Bang.

Gaia's head jerked away from the monitor at the sudden noise.

He suppressed a grin. Desired effect achieved. "I'll be out in the living room if you need anything," he said.

"Wait." She stared at him. "Let me ask you something."

Finally, he thought. As coolly and casually as he could, he shifted his position to face her. "Shoot."

"I'm just curious." She bit her lip. For once in her life, Gaia Moore actually looked unsure of herself. Incredible. "Are things getting really serious between you and . . . you know. . . ."

47

He shrugged. "I guess."

Gaia didn't say anything. The words hung thickly in the air. That was it, Ed realized. That marked a turning point. With that response, he had defined Heather. Period. And so he had also slammed the door on any vague hopes of a romance with Gaia. Not that she ever gave him a second thought, anyway. But still . . . the readiness to admit to a relationship surprised him. He didn't even think he was trying to make Gaia mad.

Well. Maybe just a little.

"Oh," Gaia said finally. Her voice was toneless. She turned back to the computer.

Ed took his cue to leave.

SAM MOON CIRCLED THE TINY,

garbage-strewn cell that was his dorm room one more time. Finally he came back to his computer. The message was still there.

Meet me at La Focaccia. We need to talk.

At first he thought it was

A Serial–Killer Sort of Way

some kind of hallucination brought on by pulling an all-nighter. But it wouldn't go away. It swirled in a jumble around his head.

Sam. Gaia. We. Future.

It was hard enough imagining those four words together in one e-mail, let alone that they could be written by Gaia herself. How could she suddenly change her mind after she learned the truth about his wasted, drunken night with Ella?

He could barely even think of Ella's name without cringing. She was so many things: a nightmare, Gaia's ridiculously young foster mother, a delusional stalker. No matter how hard he tried to stay away from her, she just wouldn't take no for an answer. She was a lunatic.

She might also be an attempted murderer.

Sam's stomach tightened into a ball. He didn't have proof, of course. Not directly. But Mike Suarez, one of Sam's suite mates and closest friends, had recently OD'd on heroin. Now he was in a coma, hooked up to life support. A college guy overdosing on drugs wasn't much of a news story to most people, but Sam knew that this one didn't ring true. Mike wasn't a junkie. He was as clean and straight as they came. It just didn't make sense.

Then Ella, as subtle as a freight train, had dropped a hint that she was the one who had injected Mike with the drug . . . all because Sam hadn't returned her advances. Of course, she didn't phrase it in those words. Oh, no. She was too smart. In a serial-killer sort of way. But the message was clear. At least in Sam's mind—

There was a light knock on the door.

"Come in," he muttered

Brendan, Sam's other suite mate, pushed open the door. He looked almost as tired as Sam felt. His eyes were puffy. His face was pale.

"Hey, man," he murmured. "Just thought I'd come by and give you the latest on Mike."

Sam nodded, swallowing. "Have there been any changes?" he asked. His voice was hoarse, shaky.

Brendan shook his head. "He's still the same. I was thinking about going over to the hospital this afternoon. You want to come?"

I should go, Sam said to himself. But he couldn't. Not with that e-mail. No. Nothing could prevent him from missing an opportunity to set things straight with Gaia—not even his crushing guilt over Mike's coma. He felt his chest tightening. He didn't even want to *think* about what kind of person that made him. It was best not to think at all. It was best just to act on his instincts and worry about the consequences later. To risk everything. Like in chess . . .

"I was thinking about going around one," Brendan prodded.

"I—I . . . wish I could go with you," Sam finally stammered. "But there's something I've got to deal with today. Maybe later."

Brendan shrugged. "That's cool. I'll see you around." He closed the door.

For a brief second Sam was half tempted to confess the truth to Brendan. The *entire* truth: Ella, Gaia, Heather, everything. The secrets were tearing him up inside. But he realized something. The truth was simply too far-fetched. Brendan probably wouldn't even believe him.

Sam sighed loudly. All that mattered now—for the next few hours, anyway—was confronting Gaia. He'd worry about Mike later. When he could. Gaia was the priority. He'd messed up so many times with her . . . but just maybe his mistakes weren't beyond the realm of forgiveness. The e-mail seemed to indicate that she wanted to give him another chance. Sam knew he didn't deserve it—but if she was willing to forgive, there was no way he was going to be stupid enough to talk her out of it.

It's fate, Sam told himself.

He almost laughed. Funny. Three months ago he would have said that there was no such thing as fate. Now he lived his life by it. Now he was as superstitious as they came.

GAIA GAPED AT THE COMPUTER

screen. Her first thought was
that some computer bug had
scrambled Ella's e-mail. But she
knew that was just wishful thinking. Actually, it was desperation,
rage, and shock all balled into
one big punch in the face. But

House of Sleaze

she read the words out loud to herself, anyway—just
to be sure this was reality and not some ludicrous
nightmare.

"Meet me at La Focaccia at 1:00 P.M. We need to
talk about our future together."

The words hung in Ed's darkened and cluttered little spare room.

Gaia almost laughed out loud. Sam and Ella.
Whatever sordid business had gone on
between them was far from over. Well.
Gaia blinked. That was what she got for hacking
into Ella's e-mail, wasn't it? The most ironic thing
about it was that she wasn't even *thinking* of Sam
when she decided to snoop on Ella. Not this time,
anyway. She just wanted to see if Ella's e-mail
would give her a clue about Ella's condition and
whereabouts.

I can't believe this is happening.

Sam—the one bright light that Gaia had always
imagined slicing through the gruesome fog that

constantly surrounded her, the only person to whom she'd even been willing to sacrifice her virginity (yes, her *virginity*)—had slept with Ella. The Wicked Witch of the West Village. The bane of Gaia's existence. A woman practically twice Sam's age to boot.

Of course, Gaia had known this for about a week now. But seeing the evidence here, again, *now* . . . Well, one thing was very clear. Her foster mother was a woman who took immense pleasure in inflicting maximum pain.

This is the woman Sam chooses to sleep with. Instead of me.

Gaia grabbed the mouse and hastily exited Ella's e-mail. Her fingers began to shake. A terrible, hot sensation was filling her chest. The thing was, the sex wasn't even the worst of it. No. The worst of it was that this obviously meant more to Sam than just some cheap fling. He was e-mailing her. Making plans. Apparently he thought they had a "future together."

Maybe he was even in love.

Gaia dropped her head to the desk, burying her face in her shivery arms. Her eyes burned with tears she refused to shed. Her insides were splintering like shards of window glass. Why had she even allowed herself to get in a position where she could be hurt by a guy? Those kinds of problems were for normal people, with normal lives. Not mutant orphan freaks with overdeveloped muscles.

One thing was abundantly clear, though. She had to leave. She had to find her uncle Oliver. Immediately. Staying at Ed's would only prolong the agony. Yes . . . deep in her core, Gaia knew that the smart thing to do was to just walk away. Let the two sleazoids have each other. They could have a sleazy wedding and make sleazy babies together and live in a house of sleaze, if they wanted.

But sensibility was quickly eclipsed by the white-hot fire ripping through Gaia's veins. She wasn't about to let go so easily. No. Why let them have all the fun? Why not give them both a piece of her mind before she split town and never saw them again?

Right. She stood up straight, tightening her fists at her side. It was time to confront them both.

TOM MOORE WATCHED THE TALL,

somber nurse glide in from the hallway to change his wound dressings. Covert government hospitals had a concrete

Small Consolation

minimalism that had a way of making regular hospitals seem like luxurious resort hotels. The windowless walls were painted pigeon gray. The air was as thick and damp as a basement. The only fixture in the room that provoked any interest was the ten-inch TV set mounted in the corner. It was muted, displaying satellite-fed news from around the globe.

"If it gets really bad, let me know," the nurse said. "I'll bring more painkillers."

Tom nodded. He still couldn't believe that in all the confusion, Ella had managed to get off a shot. Even more astounding was that the shot had actually *hit* him. But he shouldn't bother concerning himself with that right now. It was a waste of time. What mattered was that he was able to escape the scene without any police involvement.

Of course, he still owed an explanation to the Agency. And he knew that the Agency could not have been happy with his recent . . . activity.

He was supposed to be on assignment in Russia. He was supposed to be working to thwart a terrorist network. Instead he'd devoted the past month to spying on his daughter. And he'd even managed to compromise *that* . . .

The nurse began to remove the bandages.

Tom glanced at the dark, clotted hole in his arm. *Gaia saw me.*

It never should have happened. On the other hand, she would have been killed. Tom swallowed at the memory of her haunted eyes, meeting his across that chaotic street. Eyes that searched and yearned for answers.

He winced. The pain of that memory was far greater than that of this bullet hole.

Every day of his life he ached to have his daughter back. To take her in his arms and tell her how sorry he was for leading the kind of life that threatened her safety and happiness. For leaving her to take on the whole world by herself . . .

Tom stared blankly at the television, his eyes glazing over. He could only imagine what Gaia must have thought of him. She had always been so head-strong and opinionated. It was bad enough that he'd left her once, but could she ever forgive him for leaving her twice? And now, on top of it all, to realize that Ella was an enemy . . . it was almost too much to bear. It was *his* fault for placing his daughter in that house.

The only small consolation was knowing he had trained Gaia supremely well in the art of self-defense. She had been able to handle herself in the past. He'd seen it. Still, would it be enough? Maybe she was in over her head. She was only a child. . . .

Propping himself up with his good arm, Tom struggled to get off the hospital bed. "I have to get out of here," he said with a groan. "I have to—"

"You're not going anywhere," the nurse interrupted, gently but firmly. "Not right now, anyway. There's too great a risk of infection. Give it a day. At the very least."

He struggled against her, a hot sweat breaking out on the surface of his skin. He teetered for a moment as the searing pain radiated up his arm and throughout his chest—then collapsed on his pillow in exhaustion.

"But I need to see my daughter," he croaked.

The nurse wrapped the clean bandage around his shoulder. "You're not going anywhere," she repeated.

Tom's jaw tightened. He knew he couldn't argue. He *couldn't* go anywhere. But in a day, there was a very good chance that Gaia would be dead.

Alternate Universe

LA FOCACCIA WAS PACKED WITH A lunchtime crowd of hip, art gallery types—men in dark suits, skinny women in designer dresses, bags of bones, really . . . people with whom Ella might have associated in an alternate universe. She shook her head as she followed the hostess through the sea of tables. The downtown art scene couldn't provide the same thrills that Loki had. That was for damn sure. Yet there was a certain dignity in leading an honest life. Wasn't there?

Of course, the real question was this: How many of these people were actually *honest*?

Ella smirked. She knew enough about human nature to know that very few human beings could fit that description. In a way, Ella was more honest than any of them. She followed her desires.

And she was about to follow them again. The hostess—a pretty, petite woman with long black hair—motioned toward a red leather, horseshoe-shaped booth. It was nestled in a cozy back corner. Very romantic. The kind of booth where young lovers nuzzled each other while their dinners grew cold. Ella's stomach tingled as she slid into her seat. Once again, Sam Moon had miraculously stepped in to save her from her miserable sham of a life. Too bad Gaia couldn't be here with them to see it. Maybe Ella should videotape it and send her a copy. Gaia could have her dear uncle Loki, but Ella would have Sam. Ella would be the winner. And Gaia would know it. She *had* to know it—

"Can I get you a drink while you wait?" the hostess asked.

Ella nodded brusquely. "A glass of red wine," she stated. "Oh—and I'm expecting someone. A young man. His name is Sam Moon. Can you send him this way when he arrives?"

"Certainly." The hostess smiled, then turned and left. Ella eased back in the cushions. There were so many plans to make. Now that Sam had finally come to his senses, the execution of those plans was going to be a lot more smooth. First, Ella would divorce George—a given—and then she and Sam would get the hell out of the country. Maybe Paris. Definitely somewhere in Europe. Because after a few blissful weeks together, they would turn to business. They would hunt down Loki and Gaia. They would have their revenge. They would be like . . . what? A modern-day Bonnie and Clyde? Something along those lines . . .

It was going to be so beautiful.

A minute later the waitress returned with a large glass of merlot.

"Thank you," Ella murmured. She took a long, deep sip—savoring the heavy liquid as it filled her stomach with a delicious warmth. Her mind was spinning wild with possibility. *Hurry up, Sam,* she thought impatiently. *Everything depends on you.*

GAIA RAN ACROSS FOURTEENTH

Street into Union Square Park, her long, muscular legs pumped full of anger and adrenaline. It was farmers' market day, which meant a poky crowd of shoppers was

Melting Pot of Gawkers

meandering through the maze of tents at maddeningly slow speeds, weighing heavy decisions like whether they should buy a bouquet of wildflowers or a freshly baked apple pie.

What would life be like if *that* was the hardest decision *she* had to make?

Whatever. Gaia shook the question from her mind as she darted through the crowd. On most days she made a point of circumventing the entire scene, but the quickest way to La Focaccia was through the park. She didn't want to be late. Not for this.

A speech of sorts hummed through her mind, fragments and digs she wanted to get in when she finally had the chance to confront Sam and Ella together. But all she could seem to think of were lame clichés, scenes out of made-for-TV romance movies, like, "You disgust me," and, "I hope you both rot in hell." Still, those could be keepers. Gaia even toyed with the idea of violence. She was open to a little spontaneity.

The real satisfaction, though, was going to be in seeing the look of utter shock on their faces when she walked in. Gaia didn't care if it was dangerous. How could she? She was fearless. Ella could do anything. Pull a gun. Attack with kung fu. Call the police. Whatever happened, the confrontation was going to be worth it.

Gaia picked up her pace, dodging booths of plants and fruit and baked goods. A bulldog on a leash darted unexpectedly in front of her path. She vaulted the animal smoothly, hardly missing a step. For a moment she almost smiled. Soon she would be there. Soon she would extract her revenge.

From several yards away, Gaia's acutely sensitive ears began picking up the tuneless strumming of the old blind Caribbean man who sang and played guitar in the middle of the market. She had seen him there a couple of times before. He always sat on the same rickety folding chair, his red-velvet-lined guitar case open to receive donations from passing shoppers. His voice was as flat and lazy as his guitar playing—but his music had an easy, lovable style to it. As far as Gaia was concerned, the old guy's singing was the best thing the farmers' market had to offer. Well, that and those oversized, homemade chocolate chip cookies.

As she rounded a corner to the blind guy's usual spot, Gaia saw that he'd managed to attract a small crowd. A crowd of two, actually: a boy and a girl—each about twelve years old. Usually people ignored him or dropped change in the open guitar case and hurried away. But these two were standing right in front of him.

Wait a second. Gaia slowed to a trot. Her eyes narrowed.

The girl had a backpack and a heavy down parka. She kept poking the boy urgently in the ribs with her elbow, as if she was urging him to do something. The boy scratched the top of his black wool hat, his eyes glued to the guitar case full of money. Gaia's gaze flashed to the blind guy. He kept on playing, completely unaware of the pair. Oh, shit. It didn't take a member of the CIA to figure out what kind of scene was unfolding.

Gaia came to a full stop. She was less than fifteen feet away from the three of them. The two kids had their backs turned to her.

The boy looked over one shoulder. Then he looked back down at the money.

Oh, come on, Gaia pleaded silently. *Don't do it.*

Maybe her words would somehow cross the distance and seep into the kid's subconscious mind. It was strange. Not so long ago she would have actually *welcomed* a sight like this, actually gone *looking* for just such a situation—one where jerks like these kids preyed on the helpless and the weak. Because then she could take care of them. She had even gone so far as to circle Washington Square Park in the wee hours of morning, trying to look like a helpless victim in order to lure muggers out of the shadows and into her fists. After all, if she was a freak, why not put that to good use?

But right now . . . now was not the time.

The boy took a step closer to the guitar case.

Don't do it.

Gaia knew she couldn't just sit by when she saw something happen. If the kid *did* take the money, she would have to chase him down. She was involved now. There was no turning back. She just wished she hadn't noticed.

Don't make me late. . . .

But Gaia's silent pleas never reached the kids. The girl in the silver parka gave the boy another nudge. That was all it took. Quick as a flash, the boy bent down and greedily snatched the cash out of the guitar case. Change dropped everywhere as he tried to shove the money into the pockets of his oversized jeans. The guitar player stopped playing and singing.

"Hey!" somebody in the crowd yelled.

The boy and girl flinched—then broke into a fevered sprint, heading across the park lawn.

It was amazing how two little juvenile delinquents could be surrounded by hundreds of onlookers and still manage to get away. Gaia shook her head. That was New York City. A big, filthy, melting pot of gawkers. She exhaled tiredly and took off after them.

"ELLA?"

Ella looked up from her wineglass to see the curvy figure of a blond in an expensively tailored suit and pearl choker.

"Pearl?"

Schoolgirl Crush

A smile spread across her face. In all the unbelievable drama of the past twenty-four hours, she'd almost forgotten meeting this woman just the other day while shopping at the Frederick's sale. But now the memories came flooding back. Of course, some were clearer than others. The two had bonded instantly over trashy lingerie and then proceeded to swap stories over drinks . . . many, many drinks. But even in her stupor, Ella had been certain that they were kindred spirits. Pearl was smart, classy, and pulled together. Pearl was someone to admire.

"This is so funny!" Pearl exclaimed. "I just finished having lunch with a client."

Ella nodded. She felt a strange stirring in her chest. Lunch with a client. It all sounded so *normal*. But glamorous at the same time. The way *her* life should be . . .

"You're not having lunch all by yourself, are you?" Pearl asked, pursing her lips.

"No, no." Ella laughed, then scooted to the opposite end of the horseshoe to make room. "I'm meeting someone. Do you have time for a quick drink?"

"Sure." Pearl slid gracefully into the booth.

A waiter instantly appeared. "Can I get you something?" he asked.

"Just water," Pearl replied. She winked at Ella. "I have to work this afternoon."

Ella grinned, then raised her wine. "That never stopped me. . . ."

Pearl laughed. The sound of it was so sweet and controlled, like music. "So, I thought we were supposed to get together again. Why didn't you give me a call?"

Ella took a sip, then tapped the stem of the glass with her long, red fingernails. Suddenly she realized that she was so sick of these stupid clawlike nails—she could barely dial the telephone with them. When she took control of her life again, they were going to be one of the first things to go. "I . . . uh." She closed her mouth, debating what to say. Then she decided the hell with it: She would just tell the truth. Or at least *part* of the truth. "I guess you could say I've been in the middle of a personal crisis," she murmured, taking another sip.

Pearl's flawless features creased with concern. "What's going on?"

"I've decided to divorce my husband," Ella stated, placing the glass back on the table. "I'm starting over." *Which is pretty much true,* she added silently.

"Good lord." Pearl's eyes widened. "When did you decide that?"

"Just now."

For an instant their gazes met. Then they both smiled. Pearl leaned forward and covered Ella's hand with hers.

"Don't worry, Ella," she whispered. "I've been through the divorce mill a few times myself. I know how painful it can be—though the settlement *always* has a way of easing the sting."

Ella laughed in spite of herself. Pearl never said the wrong thing. Ever. She was utterly fabulous. The kind of person Ella could be. The kind of person Ella was *meant* to be.

"It's not that bad, really," Ella admitted after a

moment. "The truth of it is . . . well, I guess I never loved George." She sighed. "The situation's kind of complicated."

Pearl raised her eyebrows conspiratorially. "Another man?" she whispered.

Surprisingly, Ella's face suddenly grew warm. She knew she must be blushing. In a way, she almost felt like a schoolgirl with a crush. But that was okay. It was *pure* somehow.

"You don't have to tell me," Pearl said with a laugh. She withdrew her hand.

"No, no . . . it's just, I don't know." Ella smiled. The wine was beginning to make her dizzy.

"He's a college student," she found herself confessing. "He's the one I'm meeting here today."

Approval glinted in Pearl's topaz eyes. "A college guy? Hmmm. Very tasty."

There was a tone in Pearl's voice that was so comforting—as if she were inviting Ella to reveal all of her secrets. She was someone who would never judge Ella. Not like Loki or George or Gaia. No. Pearl was someone who would understand Ella. A friend.

"I don't know why, but I feel like I could tell you anything," she whispered.

Pearl blinked. "Is that right? How nice."

Without warning, Ella felt herself letting go. Maybe it was the wine, or the stress, or Loki's betrayal, or almost getting shot . . . but she no longer had any control over her emotions. "I've been pretending, Pearl," she blurted out. "I've been pretending to be someone else. I've been dressing differently, cutting my hair differently, marrying a man I don't even love, all because the man I was in love with told me to do it. . . ." Tears welled up in her eyes. It had been so long since she'd cried. Too long.

"Shhh," Pearl soothed. "It's all right."

"No, it's not," Ella choked out. "It's never all right."

That deathly
figure in
the doorway
was just
another
Skizz—a
vampire that
sucked the
blood of the
living.

too
late

and the boy with the oversized jeans sprinted across Union Square East just as the traffic light changed. Gaia hung back on the park side, letting the yellow cabs fill in the gulf between them. If it had been any other day, she probably would've

The Biggest Idiot on the Planet

dodged the rush of vehicles to keep up with them. But not today. There was no way Gaia was going to risk personal injury—and the possibility of missing Sam and Ella's private party for two—for a couple of punk-ass twelve-year-olds.

When the light changed again, Gaia bolted down Sixteenth Street. The pair hadn't gotten very far. The silver parka loomed less than a half block ahead, in the doorway of a four-story brownstone. As Gaia gained on them, she could see a man standing in the doorway, wearing a pair of dirty jeans and a trench coat. He was sickly thin, with skin as white as bleached paper. Wide-eyed and shaking, the boy handed over the wad of stolen cash in return for a small paper bag.

A drug deal.

Gaia stiffened. Her legs continued to run, but her

body went cold. Drugs. Drug dealers. The
same kind of scum who had killed Mary . . .

Mary Moss had been the closest thing to a best
friend Gaia had ever had. Aside from Ed, Mary was the
only person to treat Gaia as if she were truly someone
worth getting to know—unlike everyone else (namely
Heather and the FOHs, Friends of Heather), who
treated her like a weirdo freak.

At first Gaia didn't want a friend. But Mary never
gave up on her. And it wasn't long before Gaia began
to trust her because she knew that Mary didn't want
anything from her.

Of course, that all changed when Gaia discovered that Mary had a coke habit. Mary wasn't the
happy-go-lucky, carefree girl Gaia had thought she
was but a troubled addict struggling with demons
Gaia couldn't even begin to imagine. But with
Gaia's help, Mary vowed to give up cocaine. And she
would have, too—if it weren't for Skizz, her old
drug dealer.

If it weren't for me, Gaia thought, swallowing.

Skizz had hounded Mary over an old drug debt,
threatening her life. And in turn, Gaia had
hunted Skizz down and beat him so
fiercely, she nearly killed him. She should
have killed him. *Not* killing him had been a big mistake.
Because Skizz retaliated by hiring an assassin to kill
Mary. It happened in the park. Gaia and Ed had only

been a few yards away when Mary was shot. She'd died in Gaia's arms.

Every single day Gaia had to battle with the painful memories of losing Mary—the things she should have done differently to keep her alive. Every single day Gaia dreamed about how different her life would be if Mary were still around. Sometimes she got pissed at Mary. Other times she just felt sorry for herself.

And now . . . now she just felt rage.

Yes, the numbness began to fade, replaced by a stinging mixture of anger and grief. The winter air was very cold, but her skin was hot. That deathly figure in the doorway was just another Skizz—a vampire that sucked the blood of the living. A foul creature who enslaved poor kids like Mary and these two idiots who'd robbed the blind guy. Gaia broke into a sprint.

It was too late to do anything for Mary. But it wasn't too late for these two.

Almost there . . .

Before any of them could react, Gaia barreled between the boy and the girl and hurled herself at the drug dealer, raising her left leg in a powerful jump kick. The dealer's dead eyes widened. His thin blue lips twitched in surprise as Gaia lifted herself off the ground. The next instant the bottom of her boot made solid contact with the underside of the drug dealer's chin. His skull smacked against the back of the brownstone's door. His jaw went slack. He crumpled in a heap on the stoop. Gaia landed on top of him and nearly fell down. She grabbed the door frame to keep her balance, breathing heavily, filling the air with frozen white vapor.

The kids just stared at her.

For a moment the three of them were silent. Gaia glanced down at the dealer. He was out cold but breathing. A thin trickle of blood dribbled down his chin.

"What the hell did you do that for?" the boy cried, still holding the bag. He thrust his finger at the dealer's pallid face. "You could have killed him!"

Gaia shook her head, gasping for breath. Luckily a single jump kick wasn't enough to drain her completely—unlike an extended combat. "You're getting mixed up in some bad stuff," she managed to choke out. "And you don't even know it."

The girl's face twisted in sneering contempt. "How do *you* know?"

"I've seen people get killed over it," she shot back.

"Over Pokémon cards?" the girl demanded.

Gaia blinked. *What the—*

Without thinking, she snatched the paper bag out of the boy's hands and peered inside. Holy shit. Part of her wanted to laugh. Another, much larger and more irritated part wanted to scream. And there was a third part, too . . . the part that suddenly felt very sick and ashamed that she had knocked a guy cold over ten brand-new packs of Pokémon cards.

"Well . . . well, how was I supposed to know?" Gaia sputtered. She shoved the bag back in the kid's hands. "I mean, why did you buy them from *him?*"

As if trying to answer, the guy on the ground moaned.

"He gets them wholesale," the boy spat, as if Gaia were the biggest idiot on the planet. "Bigger profit margin."

Gaia realized something at that moment. Ella was probably meeting Sam at the restaurant right now, and here she was talking about the finer points of Pokémon trading with a couple of kids. Which meant that the boy was right. She *was* the biggest idiot on the planet.

"Look, I'm sorry," she mumbled. "But it doesn't change the fact that you stole money from that guy at the farmers' market."

The boy snorted. "He doesn't even know it's gone."

"*I* know it's gone," Gaia growled. "So if you don't want to end up like your friend here, you better put that money back in the guitar case by the end of the day."

He smirked, but she could see the fear in his face.

She wasn't surprised. New York City kids always tried to act a thousand times tougher than they really were.

"And if we don't?" he asked.

"Then I'm coming after you both." Gaia stared him down. "I'll find you. And if you don't believe me, you should. I never lie."

The girl rolled her eyes and grabbed the boy's sleeve. "Come on," she said with a groan. "Let's put it back right now. We got the cards, anyway."

For a few seconds Gaia stood on the stoop, watching as the kids trudged back to the farmers' market. She didn't even know what to feel. Embarrassed? Sorry? Pissed? Maybe she shouldn't try to think about it. She'd done her good deed for the day. It was time to move on.

IF THERE WAS ONE THING PEARL

Enemies

hated, it was causing a scene.

She was beginning to see why Loki wanted this foolish woman dead. Oh, yes. People at the restaurant were starting to stare. And who could blame them? Here was Ella, slumped over a glass of red wine at one o'clock in the afternoon, bawling like an infant. "I'm so tired of being who I am," she kept sobbing. "I'm so tired of pretending. I just want to erase it all and start again. Can I do that? Can I start over?"

No, Pearl answered silently. *But I can certainly put you out of your misery.*

It was a shame, really. When they'd first met, Pearl had to admit: She'd been intrigued by Ella. Of course, professionalism prevented her from ever feeling anything more than mild contempt for her victims. But she could at least appreciate Ella's beauty. That is, when the woman's mascara wasn't running. Pearl leaned away from her in the small booth. It was time to finish this job. She reached into her Prada handbag and pulled out a clean tissue.

"Shhh," she soothed in a whispery, seductive voice. "It's okay—"

"I want to be just like you," Ella blubbered.

As if, Pearl thought, struggling not to sneer. Now the situation was getting out of hand. People might overhear this. "I think you'd better go to the ladies' room and clean up your face," she murmured with a perfectly plastic smile. "We wouldn't want your college friend to see you looking like a raccoon."

Ella nodded, sniffling like a sulky little girl. A few stray teardrops fell on Pearl's boiled wool jacket as Ella clumsily maneuvered out of the booth and fled to the bathroom. It took every ounce of Pearl's strength not to lash out at her. Loki might have been upset that

Pearl had botched the first attempt, but she'd make damn sure he paid for the dry cleaning.

Others in their profession trembled before the mighty Loki. Not Pearl. She trembled before no one. No terrorist could ever instill fear in her. Terrorists, too, were clouded by emotion. Pearl was sublimely void of feelings or attachments. Except to money, of course. She allowed herself a quick smile. And that was what made her such a success. She could be out of the country and in a dozen places with numbered bank accounts before Loki ever tried to extract some misguided revenge for failure.

Not that she had any intention of failing. Last time was nothing more than an unfortunate aberration.

Once Ella was completely out of sight, Pearl reached for the antique hair comb tucked into her French twist: an exquisite, sterling silver piece with three prongs and a fan across the top. In the center was a large pearl. It covered a hidden compartment. The comb had served her well over the years by not only being incredibly convenient but also adding just the right touch of class in the right circumstances.

Style was paramount.

Loki appreciated style, too, of course. He had *that* going for him.

Pearl tilted the comb over the wineglass and pressed the clasp. She took an instant to scan the restaurant. Nobody was looking in her direction. The pearl swung open, spilling an ultrafine white powder into Ella's wine. It was a perfect poison. Its recipe was over a thousand years old, in fact, developed in the kuji-kiri school of ninjitsu: tasteless, odorless, completely untraceable, and highly toxic. After one sip the victim's veins and arteries began to swell—severely choking off the blood supply until a vein or artery burst. In other words, the symptoms mimicked an aneurysm. Exactly. And there was no way to prove otherwise.

Pearl took out her cell phone and dialed Loki's number.

"Is she dead yet?" he asked immediately.

She decided to ignore his poor manners. "In about ten minutes," she whispered.

"Make it five," he ordered. The line went dead.

SAM GLANCED AT HIS REFLECTION

in the glass doors of La Focaccia and smoothed a few windblown ginger-colored curls away from his face. He looked okay, didn't he? Relatively calm? His heart was pounding so loud that he was certain Gaia would be able to hear it.

Bogus Message

Relax, he ordered himself. He had to keep a cool head. He should look at this encounter . . . well, like the way he looked at all potentially dangerous or stressful situations: like a game of chess. He had an opportunity here. He had to strike first. He had to make things right with Gaia. Period. Failure was not an option. He took a deep breath and marched through the door.

Inside, the restaurant was filled with stuffed shirts and other stodgy business types . . . but there was no sign of that gorgeous blond tangle of hair. His heart continued to rattle. *So she's a little late,* he told himself. *No reason to panic just yet.* It was to be expected. Gaia wasn't exactly the sort of person whose life was ruled by timetables.

The hostess greeted him with a cool smile. "Can I help you?" she asked.

"I'm meeting a friend," Sam said.

The woman's eyes seemed to narrow. "Is your name Sam Moon?"

He blinked in surprise. "Uh . . . yeah."

"Your friend is already here," she said with a smile. "Right this way."

A faint sigh of relief escaped Sam's throat as he snaked his way through the tables. He didn't want to admit it, but for a minute there . . . no. It didn't matter.

The hostess motioned toward the back corner of the room. "Right over there, in the booth."

Sam's eyes followed her direction. Then he gasped. His legs nearly gave out from under him. He was suddenly paralyzed, turned to ice.

No, no, no . . .

It wasn't Gaia in the booth. It was *Ella*—easing herself down beside some well-dressed blond woman who looked like she'd materialized right out of the society pages.

He whirled to face the hostess. But she was already gone.

This was impossible. What was Ella doing here? Had she tricked him somehow? She must have. She must have used Gaia's account to send him a bogus message. . . . His mouth went dry. His throat burned. He felt like his stomach had been dropkicked down an elevator shaft. In a way, he should have seen this coming. Ella was capable of anything. *Anything—*

All at once, his rage vanished. It was replaced instantaneously by a chill of terror.

Ella *was* capable of anything.

Which meant that Gaia *could* have sent the message. But Ella had somehow found out about it. And decided to do something about it.

I have to get out of here. . . . Sam backed away slowly against the wall, avoiding any sudden movement that might attract her attention. Sweat poured down his back. His shirt stuck to his skin. Memories flashed through his mind of the bar he had gone to just before the new year. The bar where he had met Ella for the first time. If only he could've lived that night over again . . .

Gaia might be in some kind of danger. Now. Because of *that*. It was absurd, insane.

For Christ's sake, the whole ridiculous chain of events started when Sam heard that Heather had cheated on him with Charlie Salita. How crazy was *that*? He could barely even remember what Heather looked like. Even then he knew he was in love with Gaia and not Heather. But his ego had been bruised. So he went to the park to play a little speed chess with Zolov and get his mind off things. That's when Zolov told him Gaia was in love with him. . . .

And that's when Ella entered his life. She'd answered his phone call. She'd told him that Gaia was out with her boyfriend. And when he'd idiotically decided to drown his sorrow in a bottle of vodka, that mysterious redhead had appeared before him. Looking beautiful. Seductive. She'd brought him back to a hotel room and—

"Mr. Moon, are you all right? Did you not see the booth?"

Sam flinched. The hostess had returned. He shook his head violently, unable to speak.

81

All at once the hostess smiled. "Oh, I get it," she whispered. She winked at him. "This is a blind date, isn't it? I bet you don't even know what she looks like. I'm sorry I wasn't more clear about which table was yours. Here, let me show you."

This couldn't be happening. It was some bad comedy gone awry, some nightmare from which he would awake in a matter of seconds. He had to make a run for it. Yes, if he bolted out of the restaurant, he would surely wake up. . . .

But at that moment Ella looked up and greeted him with a carnivorous grin.

"*That's* your table," the hostess said brightly, pushing him forward. "Enjoy."

"WELL, WELL, WELL," ELLA MURMURED,

her eyes roving up and down every inch of Sam's body. He'd actually dressed up for the occasion. Amazing. He was wearing khakis, a pressed shirt, a *jacket*, even. He was beyond sexy; he was priceless. Even more amazing was that the emotional breakdown

Not One, But Two

she'd just experienced was already forgotten—a thing of the past, a trivial episode to be swept under the rug. Sam was here. All was right in the world. She didn't even want to finish her wine. There was no need. She didn't want to be numb. She wanted to be wide awake, here, in the moment.

But . . . why did he look so upset? He kept staring at his shoes. He wouldn't even sit.

"He *is* delicious," Pearl whispered shamelessly.

Ella nodded. It pleased her that Pearl approved of her choice. It *vindicated* her. She cleared her throat and made some room for him. "Sam, this is my friend Pearl. She just stopped by to say hello."

Sam didn't respond. He stood as rigid as a sign-post. Maybe he was feeling shy. Who could blame him, though? Here he was, confronted not by one but by *two* beautiful women. Older women. Sophisticated women. Every boy's dream. Anyway, after dealing with Loki's aggressive, arrogant personality for so many years, shyness in a man was definitely a turn-on.

Pearl slid out of the booth and stood. "Pleased to meet you, Sam," she said with a polite smile. She extended a hand. "I was just leaving, actually," she said, sneaking Ella a quick wink.

Sam didn't take Pearl's hand. In fact, he stared at it as if it were some kind of poisonous snake.

Hmmm. Ella frowned. Her initial contentment was

beginning to falter. Why was he acting so weird? This wasn't shyness. This was *rudeness.*

"Maybe you two should have some wine," Pearl suggested teasingly, nodding toward Ella's glass. "A little merlot might help break the ice." She blew Ella a kiss and headed toward the exit. "Bye, dear."

Ella waved. "I'll call you soon. . . ."

Pearl gave Sam one last glance over her shoulder. "Nice meeting you, Sam," she called.

He didn't say a word.

Okay—clearly something was very wrong. She grabbed Sam by the wrist and tugged him down into the booth. "What's the matter with you?"

That seemed to break the spell. Finally. Sam fixed her with a hard stare.

"Where's Gaia?" he demanded.

What? Ella's face shriveled in disgust. What did she have to do with anything? Mentioning Gaia's name to start the conversation was more than a little surprising—considering *he* was the one who arranged this rendezvous to begin with. She reached for her wine, then suddenly slammed it back on the table, overcome by anger.

"Nowhere near here," she spat. "I can assure you."

"Then where?" His voice was flat, his gaze unblinking.

"I have no idea, Sam," she stated, desperately struggling to control herself. "Gone."

84

"What did you do with her?"

Ella's eyes blazed. "Not a damn thing. Gaia skipped town this morning of her own free will." The words rolled off her tongue. She was surprised at the pleasure she could take at seeing Sam's hurt expression. But he'd get over it soon enough. "I wouldn't be surprised if she was on her way out of the country by now," she added.

He swallowed. "I don't believe you."

"You want proof?" Ella laughed without humor, then draped her arm around his neck. She could feel his muscles tense. She ignored the rebuff. "Her room's all cleaned out, and her stuff is all gone," she whispered in his ear. "I scared that girl so badly, she's probably halfway across the Atlantic. I don't know why you're all hung up on her, anyway—we're here to talk about you and me. Trust me, Sam. It's just us now. We're free."

It was funny how fear suddenly disappeared when you had nothing else to lose.

drinking that wine

SO HERE THEY WERE. IN THE FLESH.
Just as she'd always envisioned.

Gaia couldn't believe how much this actually *hurt*.

Her insides churned, bathed in bitter acid. She knew she would confront this very scene. She knew it. Sam and Ella—together. Those four words had been branded upon every moment of her consciousness like a neon sign that was never turned off. But somehow to actually see Ella's slimy tentacles wrapped around him . . . it wasn't just revolting. It was a scene that approached grossness of astronomical proportions.

Gaia's chest rose and fell quickly. Her pulse increased. A lump welled in her throat. She'd never be able to forget this. She knew it. Even seconds ago a tiny and irrational part of her had been clinging to the wild hope that this could have all been some huge misunderstanding. That the e-mails were somehow fake. That Ella had made everything up. But no. God . . . what she wouldn't give to trade fearlessness for an inability to love. At least being fearless had a few perks. Falling in love never paid off. Ever.

Screw it.

She was going to take full advantage of her

condition—in a way she'd never done before. Her blood went from simmer to boil. She brazenly marched to their table and slammed her fist down on it—so hard that Ella's wineglass rattled and a few drops swished over the rim and onto the table.

Sam looked like he'd been punched. His face went pale. His hazel eyes bulged. He threw Ella's arm off his shoulders. "Gaia!"

"That's right," Gaia hissed, her voice straining. Her cracked heart thundered in her rib cage. "So I guess it's true. You *are* the scum of the earth."

Instantly he started shaking his head, his body jolting as though he had just been zapped by a cattle prod. His soft lips trembled. For a fleeting moment Gaia almost regretted the look of pain she had caused him. But not quite. Pain was her mission. She wanted to see a lot more of it.

"What are you doing here?" Ella whispered. "I thought you were gone."

Gaia forced a brittle laugh. An electric fizz filled her body, the same sensation she always got before combat. She had a fleeting vision of cracking Ella's spine across her knee—snapping it in half like a piece of bamboo—and seeing Ella's face as she shrieked in pain. "I hope you brought your gun," Gaia said. "Because you're gonna need it again."

Sam's gaze flashed between the two of them. "What's

going on?" he whispered. "What are you talking about?"

"You didn't know?" Gaia asked, staring straight at Ella. "She shot at me."

"*What?*" Sam shouted. "I don't believe—"

"Why not?" Gaia barked. "Ask her. Just go ahead and ask her."

Sam blinked at Ella. "You . . . shot Gaia?"

Ella didn't answer. Her eyes narrowed into slits.

He turned back to Gaia. "Okay, look, Gaia, please," he begged quaveringly. "This is all a big misunderstanding. I came here to meet you—"

"That's a lie," Ella interrupted. Very calmly, she turned to Sam. "Tell Gaia the truth," she commanded. "Tell her you sent me an e-mail telling me to meet you here so we could talk about our future together."

Gaia's nostrils flared. For once she found she could actually side with Ella. *That* was how completely twisted this whole scenario had become.

"But I didn't do that," Sam protested.

Without warning, Ella lurched out of the booth. "Fine," she spat. Her eyes darted between the two of them. "You kids hash it out among yourselves, okay? I have better things to do. But I'm warning you, Gaia—you can't come home. You've run away. You're no longer welcome. So you better stay out of my life."

And with that, she turned and fled.

THE MOMENT ELLA STALKED OUT

Checkmate

of the restaurant, Sam collapsed back in his seat, overcome by two simultaneous, powerful, and contradictory emotions. One was relief—relief that she was gone, relief that he could be alone with Gaia. The other was fear. Ella hadn't left to give them privacy. Ella had left because she was up to something that very well might put either one of them in danger.

But he couldn't worry about her now. He could only focus on salvaging what he could with Gaia. If that was even possible . . .

Gaia was still standing in front of the booth. Her beautiful face had turned as cold and hard as marble. She looked just about ready to walk out, too. But he couldn't let that happen. He *wouldn't*.

"I know what you must be thinking," he forced himself to whisper, looking her in the eye. He reached for her hand, desperate to make some sort of connection. Gaia recoiled, as though she had been burned. "If you just let me explain—"

"Explain *what?*" Gaia hissed. "That you slept with my foster mother?"

Sam's mouth remained open, but the breath flowed from his lungs like air out of a punctured tire. There *was* no explanation for . . . what he did. But maybe he could explain what he was doing here with Ella. At least he could account for *that*.

91

"This morning I got an e-mail from you to meet me here," he said.

Miracle of miracles, she actually sat down. But it didn't look like she was giving in. It looked like she was sitting down to block his path so he would have a harder time escaping. Her expression was hardly conciliatory. It was threatening. This really *was* like a game of chess, wasn't it? Only he had already lost, long before this move. . . .

"I never sent you an e-mail," Gaia stated simply.

"Then Ella must have sent it," Sam countered, his voice rising. "Because I got a message with your name on it. It's on my computer. I can show you."

"Don't bother." Gaia's voice wasn't cold. It was empty. Completely devoid of feeling. Somehow the emptiness was much more painful to Sam than a scream. It meant that she just didn't care.

"Listen, I wouldn't lie to you, Gaia," Sam pleaded. "I swear."

"Then why were you sitting here, all over Ella?" Gaia asked. "I mean, come on, Sam—"

"*She* was all over *me!*" Sam cried, unable to control himself.

Gaia shrugged carelessly. "Oh. I didn't realize there was a distinction."

Sam ran his fingers through his hair. This wasn't working. Of course not. He sounded impossibly lame. How could he defend himself when even *he* couldn't blame Gaia for not believing his story? Surprisingly, though, he wasn't nearly as nervous as he had been only seconds ago. It was funny how fear suddenly disappeared when you had nothing else to lose.

"Look, Ella means nothing to me," he stated. Sam flinched at the sound of his own words, which were far less eloquent than the ones rolling around feverishly in his head. "Whatever crazy stuff is going on between you two, I had absolutely nothing to do with it."

Gaia said nothing. Her eyes were distant. Was she even listening?

"Maybe I should've told you about that thing with Ella sooner, but I couldn't get the words out," he added, plowing forward desperately. "I didn't want to hurt you."

Still no response. Gaia seemed completely cut off from him in every way. So unlike every other time he'd been in her presence. From the moment they met, Sam had felt an unspoken connection with her, a bond. It was as though certain things never needed to be said between them—they were just automatically understood. Like the fact that he would never lie to her and would never do anything to hurt her. Was he crazy? Was that connection stuff only something he dreamed up? Why wouldn't she believe him now?

"Heather broke up with me. It's all over between us. I'm single now—"

"Forget it, Sam," she interrupted. Her tone softened.

She laughed once. "You know, it's funny how the imagination works."

"I'm not lying, Gaia," he insisted. "This isn't a product of my imagination—"

"I'm not talking about *you*. I'm talking about me. Because I realize now that I never knew you. All these months . . . I mean, we've just been kind of passing each other, like planes in a big sky—each going our separate ways. And I'm glad. Because I realize now that you are the most vile human being I've ever met. Everything else was just in my imagination. I actually imagined I had feelings for you. . . ."

A searing pain shot down Sam's spine. That was it. He'd blown it. He'd blown everything. To know that Gaia had felt something for him in the past . . . It was almost too much to bear. The truth had destroyed him. He might as well give up now. There was no point in going on. He'd been checkmated.

THE RESTAURANT SEEMED TO RECEDE

into the distance. Gaia stared at the tabletop, at Ella's glass of wine, sitting there before her. She felt her entire body shutting down.

It was the exact same phenomenon

Glowing Warmth

that happened at the end of an exhausting fight. First her eyesight began to dim, then her hearing faded. Her muscles and joints would weaken to the point of collapse. It lasted for only a few minutes, but for that brief time she was enveloped in a feeling of power- lessness. Of vulnerability. Of being completely exposed.

And she hated it.

Still, being powerless after a fight wasn't nearly as miserable as being emotionally powerless. As *this*. At least when someone was pounding on you, you knew it was bound to end soon and your body would eventually heal. Or you'd die. Either way, it would end.

". . . I didn't even know she was your foster mom."

Was Sam still talking? She could barely hear his voice. It was as if the painful words were being absorbed right through her pores, slipping into her bloodstream.

". . . went to a bar and got drunk . . . She just kind of appeared out of nowhere—"

"Stop," Gaia commanded, squeezing her eyes shut and slumping helplessly against the seat. "Just stop. I don't want to hear about this."

"But I want you to know, I was depressed about you and your boyfriend," Sam persisted.

Gaia's eyelids fluttered open. She scowled at

Sam. Now he was telling lies that had no *hope* of working. He was clutching at straws—bizarre ones, at that. "I don't have a boyfriend, Sam, okay? So stop. Nothing you're saying is making any sense. . . ." Waves of agony washed over her, reaching excruciating heights that rivaled even the mysterious murder of her mother. Ever since she met Sam, Gaia felt that there was a reason to go on with her miserable life. For whatever reason, Sam had given her life purpose. He'd been . . . different.

But that was just a dream—an impossible dream of somebody who didn't even exist. Sam was a lot like her father in that way. Somebody who never delivered. He had done something cheap, just like every other guy looking for a good time. Gaia knew that there was no way she could be with him now. And without Sam, there was no point in caring about anything anymore. He had been her last hope.

More than anything, Gaia wanted to deaden the pain, but her body was wide awake. Her mind was alert—refusing to enter the bliss of unconsciousness. Almost without even realizing it, she found her fingers reaching for the base of the wineglass, for that heavy red liquid. Gaia remembered her dinner with Uncle Oliver, at that expensive restaurant, and how soothing the wine had been. It had enveloped her in a glowing warmth. . . .

96

"Tell me, Gaia," Sam begged, his voice growing more and more feverish even as it faded from her senses. "What do I need to do to make you believe me? Just tell me, and I'll do it."

"Nothing," she answered, raising the glass. "There's nothing you can do."

PEARL FIERCELY KICKED THE POINTED

Death Sentence

toe of her shoe into the base of a streetlight. What the hell was Ella *doing?* She shouldn't be walking. She should be convulsing. Never, *ever* had a target escaped once, let alone twice. Pearl might understand it if her target was exceptionally clever. But Ella was an egocentric fool. Annihilating her should have been easy.

Pearl's pulse increased ever so slightly. Loki was not going to like this. At all.

She didn't fear him, of course. No. But he had powerful friends. He had an army of henchmen. Pearl was just one person . . . a freelancer, a lone operative. Sweat broke out on her forehead. She *didn't* fear him. She could always escape. But escape would end her career. Which wasn't an option.

Even as these thoughts raced through her skull, she knew that Loki was waiting for her to call to tell him the job was finished. By now he must have suspected that something was up. She couldn't call and lie to him; he'd see right through that.

No—she had to follow Ella. But she couldn't. Not just yet.

Why the hell didn't I bring a gun? Pearl wondered angrily, watching Ella's retreating form vanish among the traffic and pedestrians. It would be so easy to pump a few rounds into Ella's back and vanish before anyone even knew what was happening. . . .

The problem was that Loki's niece was still inside with Sam and that glass of poisoned wine. Loki had made it crystal clear that if anything happened to Gaia, the consequences would be dire. Sure, the chances of Gaia's drinking that wine probably weren't huge. But it was a risk Pearl couldn't afford to take. So in essence, she was faced with an impossible juggling act: Keep one person alive, and kill the other.

Pearl rushed back across the street and peered through the restaurant window. Gaia was still there and still upright. But in a flash, panic seized Pearl.

Gaia was lifting the glass to her lips.

No!

Okay. Maybe Pearl was afraid of Loki. Admitting this wasn't a sign of weakness; it was an acknowledgment of reality. The memory of Loki's menacing eyes ripped deep into her very core. She had to do something fast. Right. She grabbed her handbag and tossed it in the nearest trash can. Then she ran back into the restaurant as fast as her legs would carry her.

GAIA TILTED BACK HER HEAD AND

Coping with Loss

opened her throat, ready to drink the entire glass in one long gulp. *Please*, she whispered silently to herself. *Let the pain go away. . . .*

But as the ruby liquid flowed toward her lips, a hysterical voice shattered the dull murmur of the restaurant: "I've been mugged! Someone please help—he took my purse!"

Frowning, Gaia set down the full glass, dribbling some wine on her chin. She wiped her face with her sleeve and glanced up to see an impeccably groomed woman standing at the door. She looked frantic. Shit. Gaia really didn't want to deal with this. But against her will, adrenaline was already gushing through her system and raising her temperature—priming her senses for action. She waited a beat or two to see if someone else would pick up the slack for once, but everybody continued stuffing their faces with pasta as if nothing was happening. Typical. No one ever wanted to get involved.

Then again, no one besides Gaia was fearless.

"Hey, I know her . . . ," Sam mumbled, craning his neck at the woman.

Gaia sniffed. Her jaw tightened. Sure, he did. He'd probably slept with her. He had a thing for older women, right? Or maybe he was just lying. That was certainly a possibility, too. Pretty soon she'd find out that he wasn't even a premed student at NYU but one of those guys who salvaged books out of trash cans and sold them at the flea market on Saturdays. Whatever. Now was as good a time as any to say good-bye to Sam Moon forever. She slid out of the booth.

"Hey—where are you going?" he protested.

"Where do you think?" she muttered, without even bothering to look behind her. "I'm going to help that woman out."

Gaia was already at the door before Sam could utter another word. Maybe this was the start of her new life. Yes. Right here and now. Or a return to her old life. Her pre-Sam life, when she roamed the city, looking for a fight. Being away from Sam might have the effect of lessening the pain of his betrayal. Right now, however, it simply hurt. But it didn't lessen her resolve. She had to get as far away from Sam as she possibly could. She had to forget him.

". . . I was standing at the light, and this man bumped my shoulder," the woman was babbling, trying to catch her breath. She was clearly shaken, unable to stand still. "The bag slid down my arm—and suddenly it was gone. . . ."

A purse snatching. Gaia frowned. Yup. Another reason New York City sucked. Another reason she had to get in touch with Uncle Oliver as soon as possible and get the hell out. This woman must have been carrying some fussy little designer number that made her an especially easy target. Gaia stepped forward.

"Did you see the person who took it?" she demanded.

The woman glanced at Gaia and blinked, then shook her head. The hostess, seizing the opportunity not to be further involved, vanished back into the kitchen. Gaia resisted the temptation to snicker.

"I—I . . . don't think so," the woman stammered. "When I turned around, he was gone. Come outside— I'll show you."

At this point there was little hope that the bag would ever be recovered, but Gaia followed, anyway. The drama was a welcome distraction. Anything was a welcome distraction at this point.

The woman stopped. "I was right here at this corner. . . ."

Gaia nodded patiently as the woman ran through her

story again—but she was hardly listening. Her steely blue eyes performed a radar sweep of the immediate area. That's when she spotted a trash can on the opposite side of the street. A trash can with a purse in it. It was every mugger's favorite trick: Swipe the money; ditch the bag.

"Is your purse a black leather shoulder bag with a silver clasp?" Gaia asked.

The woman stared at her. She seemed slightly taken aback—almost suspicious. "How did you know?"

Gaia smiled, then gently took the woman's arm and led her across the street to the trash can. "Here it is," she announced, flicking aside a few ancient french fries and pulling the bag out of the garbage.

The woman's face registered some emotion between relief and revulsion. Gaia could just imagine what was going through her mind: *Taking a purse out of the trash? Eww . . .* She flashed Gaia a pained smile, then delicately took the purse between her thumb and forefinger and opened it with her other hand, touching as little as possible. She sighed deeply. "My cash is missing, but everything else seems to be in there. . . ."

"Well, that's good," Gaia said. "You're lucky. Most people never get it back at all."

The woman nodded gratefully. "I'd like to give you a little reward. I really appreciate—"

"Oh, no, please," Gaia interrupted as politely as she could. "It's no big deal. Believe me. Really. I know what it feels like to lose something."

People I Trust . . . or
Once Trusted: (a shrinking list)

5. ~~My Father~~
4. Uncle Oliver—if his phone
   worked
3. ~~Ed~~
2. ~~Sam~~
1. Myself

But there were moments—in bed when Loki had let his guard down.

a huge mistake

PEARL WAS A VERY LUCKY WOMAN.

Loki knew she probably didn't even realize *how* lucky. But that was quite all right. She was brave; he had to credit her for that. Few others would have come directly to him after failing him twice. But even that couldn't sour his mood. Pearl had already repeated the story of how Gaia had unexpectedly showed up at the restaurant, but Loki made her tell it again. The tale sang in his ears like a symphony.

Lucky

"The girl is an absolute genius!" Loki cried, clapping and beaming like a proud father. She was definitely Katia's child. And his . . . through the unfortunate vehicle of Tom, of course. But he and Tom were made of the same genetic material. The exact same stock. Gaia *was* his. She was a Moore, first and foremost.

Finally he sighed. He leaned back in the white sofa of his sparsely furnished Upper West Side apartment and glanced up at Pearl. The woman refused to sit. She looked very calm, very collected . . . except for one telltale sign: a tiny muscle in her jaw that kept twitching. She was afraid. And he drank in her fear. It was like an oasis in the desert. It sustained him. All powerful people should fear him.

"Let's get down to business," he said.

Pearl nodded wordlessly.

"As I understand it, Ella's still breathing," Loki stated. His gaze flashed to the window, to the Manhattan skyline, glittering in the twilight of the setting sun. "Is that correct?"

"Yes," she said softly.

"*Yes*," Loki repeated, imitating her meek voice. "You sound like a mouse, not a murderer. If you were in my position, what would you do?"

Pearl shrugged. The muscle twitched again.

Before she could answer, Loki reached inside his jacket and pulled out a custom-made nine-millimeter pistol. The silencer glinted in the fading sunlight. "I was thinking of putting a bullet through your skull."

"I realize I didn't deliver my part of the agreement," she stated stiffly, her poise crumbling, "but I'm sure you understand that there were extenuating circumstances—"

"I'm not an understanding man, Pearl," he interrupted. The safety latch released with a satisfying *click*.

She took a few steps back, her gaze riveted to the shiny metal in his hand. "Everything was going according to our plan," she insisted. "If Gaia hadn't shown up . . ."

He paused. "Are you blaming my niece for your mistake?"

"No."

"Good." Loki raised the gun and aimed the barrel

directly at Pearl's forehead. Pity she would make a mess on his nice hardwood floors. That was something even *she* could appreciate. "You're sweating, Pearl. It's not very ladylike—"

"Give me another chance!" Pearl cried. "No one is closer to Ella than me right now. I have an idea that absolutely *cannot* fail."

Loki hesitated . . . then lowered his arm by his side. Well. Hiring another assassin *would* be an inconvenience. As would cleaning this place up after he killed her. So he'd wait—then kill her after the job was done. Yes. She was lucky enough to have caught him in a good mood. She probably didn't even know *how* lucky.

"Let's hear it," he said.

ELLA BLEW THROUGH THE PERRY

Street brownstone with a force that rattled every hinge and musty floorboard. But in spite of her flailing limbs  and pounding feet, in spite of her wild fantasies of smashing Gaia's smarmy little face with an ax, a part of her mind was surprisingly calm. It was the part that

108

pictured Loki's cold, arrogant eyes. The time had come to make him pay—to make them *all* pay. Loki. Gaia. Sam.

But now there would be hell to pay. For all of them.

"You don't control my life anymore," Ella whispered. Her words drifted off the walls of George's office, off the glass doors of his antique bookcases. Loki thought he'd molded her into some sort of puppet that couldn't think for herself. One of his minions. And maybe he had, in the past. Which was all well and good. That's precisely what she wanted him to believe about the present.

He was powerful, and he'd controlled her. Yes . . . she had to admit that to herself. She remembered thinking only very recently that she craved him the way an addict craved a drug. She was powerless to resist. But not anymore.

Bending over beside George's desk, she reached into the unused fireplace, her frantic hand feeling along the inside of the chimney. Shit . . . she was actually shaking. She *was* nervous. But this was a momentous occasion. Finally her fingers touched the familiar inner ledge and grazed a small iron box.

Her heart caught in her throat. It was still there.

My way out.

Shaking, she placed the soot-covered box on

the floor, then gingerly opened the top. A smile spread across her face. The contents were still in perfect condition. Inside were handwritten copies of the passwords to a few of Loki's numerous bank accounts, stashed in strategic locations around the globe. But some of the accounts, if transferred properly, could be accessed in this very city . . . from a foreign bank, maybe—like the Bank of Switzerland in Midtown or the Bank of Tunisia in Gramercy Park. It was all a matter of being clever.

Loki had been excruciatingly protective of his money. But there were moments—in bed—when Loki had let his guard down. No doubt these weren't his biggest stashes. He was too smart to reveal everything to her.

Still, Ella had found all sorts of subtle ways of finding out what she needed to know.

Of course, she never believed that a day would come when she'd actually *use* these passwords. She liked to think of them only as insurance. Something she would turn to when disaster struck. In fact, Loki had given her the information as protection in case he was killed.

It was kind of ironic, wasn't it?

No, it was something far more meaningful than ironic. It was life threatening.

110

A violent shudder seized her entire body. She swallowed. Her fingers were moist as she removed the papers. This *was* undeniably scary. Crossing Loki in this way would ensure that she became a marked woman. But she didn't care. If she stayed here—trapped in this house, in this life—well, then she would die, too.

Thrusting fear aside, Ella sat down at George's desk. Her fingers flew over the keyboard, logging on to the Internet and accessing the offshore accounts. Furiously she pounded out Loki's account information . . . followed by her own—moving quickly for fear of losing the sliver of courage that rage had granted her.

Loki would know immediately it was her. But then again, she wanted him to know.

Amount to transfer: $300,000.

Ella gazed at the screen. Her soot-covered finger hovered over the enter key. It trembled like a leaf in the wind. All that remained was a press of a single button. Then the theft would be complete. *This could be a huge mistake.* She closed her eyes and inhaled deeply, forcing herself to remember the smitten look on Sam's face when Gaia walked into the restaurant. If she didn't go through with this, she'd never be free. Of anyone.

Ella hit the key.

THERE WAS NO DOUBT ABOUT IT. UNCLE
Oliver's cell phone number was definitely not working. Gaia slammed down the pay phone receiver for the tenth time and retrieved her change as it clanged into the coin return. So

Nervous Breakdown

much for his promises to take her away from this hell-hole. For now, it looked like she was stuck here. She grabbed the box of Krispy Kreme doughnuts and took a seat at a table near the window, watching the traffic on Eighth Street pass by.

The sidewalk was packed with the usual rush of college girls—carrying heavy shopping bags, laughing, talking about spring break, or finals, or whatever the hell it was that college girls talked about when they were together. There were clusters of boys hanging out together, too. Some smiled at the girls. Some did more. Some whistled, even. How cheesy was that? But the girls flirted back. To Gaia, watching the mating rituals of college kids was like watching a documentary about orangutans on The Discovery Channel. It was equally as foreign and mysterious—but primitive and ridiculous, too.

Did anyone ever end up in a real relationship?

And when it was finally over, did the broken-hearted women of the world drown their sorrows in a warm box of Original Glazed Krispy Kreme doughnuts?

If not, they should. Gaia bit into the first doughnut slowly, savoring its sweet perfection. She didn't have a father, a home, or even Sam, but she always had Krispy Kreme doughnuts. Doughnuts were a lot more reliable than people. As far as she could tell, in fact, people were shit. Well, except for the ones she invented in her head. Like the fake Sam Moon.

Yup. The Sam Moon she had fabricated in her mind was perfect. He was smart and rational. He lived by his own code. He wasn't impressed by flash or money. (Well, barring the regrettable exception of Heather Gannis, of course. But the fake Sam never even really *liked* Heather, right?) He had a brain for chess. He was loyal. Trustworthy. Nice to everybody, even to Gaia, when everyone else wrote her off . . .

Most of all, the Sam that Gaia had dreamed up was honest.

Too bad he didn't exist.

The Sam Moon that existed in reality had the same complicated hazel eyes and face—and the same head for chess—but that was where the similarities ended. The real Sam was calculating and manipulative. Weak. Spineless. Ruled

113

by his groin. He was self-serving and callous. In short, he was a big, fat card-carrying member of Liars Anonymous.

So if the real Sam was such an asshole, then why did the thought of him still hurt so damn much?

You haven't had enough doughnuts yet—that's why, Gaia reasoned as she stuffed a second doughnut down into the empty void where her heart once was. Getting Sam out of her mind was going to be brutal. But Gaia was prepared. She'd clean out the entire Krispy Kreme inventory if she had to.

As she nibbled the icing off her third doughnut, a burst of iridescent red hair caught the corner of her eye. The shade was very particular, an amalgam of bad dye jobs ranging from fuchsia to candy apple . . . blended into a color so hideous, it was nearly radioactive.

Gaia would know that red anywhere. It belonged to Ella.

Could it be that the psychobitch was laying another trap for Gaia? Probably. Gaia licked her sugared fingers absently as Ella passed the window—not more than four feet away. She didn't look up, though. She didn't notice Gaia. But Gaia noticed *her*—specifically, that Ella looked like *crap*. The requisite Barney's shopping bag was there, but everything else was completely skewed. The eyes

114

that were normally made up were now puffed with dark circles. Hair that was normally coiffed looked like it hadn't been combed in at least thirty minutes.

Maybe Ella was having a nervous breakdown.

No. She was setting a trap for Gaia. There was no other logical explanation. It was simply too coincidental that she would walk *right* past the window where Gaia was eating. But that didn't matter. If Ella was laying a trap, Gaia figured she better find out what it was.

At least it would take her mind off Sam.

SAM WANDERED AIMLESSLY PAST

One Last Thing to Say

Astor Place, choosing to avoid the crush of lower Broadway by sticking to the wide, desolate sidewalks of Lafayette. Even at rush hour this was one of the few avenues in Manhattan that wasn't jammed with a steady stream of cabs, buses, and pedestrians. And every few minutes, in between lights, the air was actually quiet enough to allow a person to think.

Not that Sam was *capable* of thinking. Even if he were in a library—no, better yet, even if he were in one of those isolation tanks where people succumbed to hallucinations because it was so freaking quiet—even *then* he wouldn't be able to think. The only thing he could do right was walk. One foot in front of the other. Over and over again. Just like a fish that had to keep moving to breathe. If he stopped for even a second, Sam felt he might die.

Strange: He used to walk all the time. Back when he was happy. Relatively happy, anyway. How long ago had *that* been? Four months? Six? Life had once been pretty good. Or at least halfway decent. He had an NYU scholarship, good friends, and a hot girlfriend that made him the envy of all his suite mates. Things were fairly uncomplicated. He knew where he was going and where he was likely to end up. All the pieces of his life had a way of fitting together. Perfectly.

Like a chess game.

But then he met Gaia.

As soon as he caught a glimpse of that tangled blond hair and those brooding blue eyes, Sam felt stirrings of discontentment gnawing at his insides. Something was suddenly *missing*. He couldn't put his finger on it, either. No. But nothing seemed to satisfy him anymore. He couldn't study. He zoned out whenever he was with his friends. Heather started feeling more like a burden than a girlfriend. Everything that had once mattered to him before no longer had any real meaning.

And *why?* That was the kicker. He had no idea. No goddamn idea whatsoever. It wasn't as if he ever spent any long, meaningful periods of time with Gaia. Not like he had with Heather. His infatuation made absolutely no sense.

But still, he was sure that Gaia had to be in his life. Even though there was clearly no place for her. She was like the extra piece you find in the puzzle box that you don't know how to use when you've put everything else together. So Sam started pushing things aside, fighting to make her fit—any way he could. And his life started falling apart in the process.

First his grades went down the tubes. Heather broke up with him, but that was to be expected. His friends started hanging out with him less—and then came that whole whacked-out situation with Mike being in the hospital. . . .

He almost stumbled. Shit. He should really go see Mike. But he just couldn't bring himself to do it. Facing *that* reality was too much to handle.

Why couldn't he make his life work?

Sam brushed past Tower Discount, his head bowed toward the sidewalk. The most maddening part of it all was that it could have happened with Gaia. It *should* have happened. Or maybe it was never supposed to happen at all. Maybe he was destined to not spend the rest of his life with Gaia but only to chalk her up as a great learning experience. Maybe a straitlaced guy like him was only supposed to be with an outgoing, predictable sort of girl . . . somebody who went for designer clothes and celebrity gossip.

Someone like Heather.

No. He was lying to himself.

He stopped and leaned against the doorway of a small vintage clothing boutique. His head swam with regret and lost possibilities. It was beyond too late to explain himself and his inexcusable actions or to even apologize. But there was still one last thing he needed to say to Gaia.

She could go on hating him for the rest of her life if she wanted to, but he had to say it.

He had to tell Gaia that he loved her. *Now.*

Sam sucked in a burst of clear air. Then he turned around and sprinted toward Washington Square Park.

Gaia caught the briefest flash of Ella's eyes in the darkness. She could see the whites. **ritual** There was terror there. Ella knew she was about to die.

GAIA TRAILED SEVERAL YARDS BEHIND
Ella, her mane of
hair strategically tucked
under her black wool cap.
The first rule of surveillance, as her father had
taught her, was to hide
one's most distinguishing
feature.

Post-apocalyptic B Movie

But tagging Ella
wasn't quite the easy
errand Gaia had hoped for—certainly not as easy
as the last time. Maybe this *wasn't* a trap. Part of
the problem was that Ella seemed to have a total
indifference to traffic signals. She frequently
walked through a rush of speeding cabs and buses,
yet somehow managed to avoid impact. She had
excellent reflexes. Not that this was a big shocker
to Gaia. Behind Ella's mask of complete
obliviousness and utter self-
absorption lurked a trained martial
artist . . . a walking weapon. Like Gaia
herself.

Clearly Ella had somewhere important to be. The
question was *where?* Gaia had already followed her
through the Village and SoHo, half expecting Ella to
stop at any number of posh coffee bars or trendy shops
geared toward teenage fashion (the stepmonster's

favorite), but none of them so much as turned her head. Weird.

They continued moving south toward Canal . . . toward Chinatown. This was definitely stretching the boundaries of Ella's comfort zone. The neighborhood tended to get a little sketchy down here unless one stuck to the busy thoroughfares that were always packed with tourists. Maybe Ella was going to meet someone. Maybe she was going to sit around one of those communal tables at Joe's Shanghai, slurping a bowl of noodles. . . .

Ella turned left on Canal Street, then quickly made a right on Pell. Gaia kept after her. The pungent odor of fish, medicinal herbs, and fried noodles permeated the air. No sunlight reached the crowded street; it was too narrow, and the buildings were too close together. The thickly populated sidewalk hid Gaia from view. She got a bit closer as Ella slithered her way past sidewalk booths filled with sunglasses and T-shirts, swinging her Barney's bag at her side. Even with so many people crammed together on the street, Ella's steps never once slowed or hesitated. She was definitely on a mission. . . .

At last Ella ducked into an unremarkable doorway.

Gaia waited for a moment, counted to ten, then walked past the stoop. She couldn't help but frown. The name of the store was Mr. Chin's Trading Post.

Its front window was filled with stacks of ancient television sets. Everything was covered in dust. It looked like Mr. Chin hadn't sold a piece of equipment since before Gaia was born.

So. Maybe it was a front.

Sure. Gaia had seen businesses like this before scattered all over the city: small, unkempt storefronts with dirty windows that displayed prehistoric merchandise. Or sometimes the stores seemed slightly more legitimate, stocking their meager shelves with a few rolls of film, gum, and maybe a soda cooler . . . but there were never any customers. They all looked like scenes out of some postapocalyptic B movie. Obviously there was no way these stores survived on the merchandise. They had to be a cover for illegal backroom operations.

Gaia turned at the end of the block, then hung outside a restaurant, trying to look casual. A tingle of energy shot through her veins. She might be on the verge of stumbling onto a clue that would solve the mystery of Ella. Drug smuggling, arms dealing, black market breast implants—what exactly was she up to?

Then again, there was a very good chance that Ella had lured Gaia down here simply to kill her. If Gaia had learned anything, it was never to underestimate the woman. Ever.

IT HAD BEEN A LONG, LONG TIME

Impression of Luxury

since Ella had stepped into this place.

She couldn't help but be mildly repulsed. The good life with George had . . . well, it had long shielded her from the more seamy

undersides of the city. *That* had been a benefit, she supposed. Yes. It definitely had. Perry Street wasn't all bad. There had always been a bottle of good, expensive wine available, after all.

But this was not the time to reminisce.

Ella leaned against the scratched wooden counter and stared at the only other person on the premises: a shriveled old woman reading a Chinese newspaper. Ella didn't recognize her, but that meant nothing. The man who operated this "business" undoubtedly used many different buffers to keep outsiders away from him. Ella coughed once. The woman didn't seem to notice. The dust in this place was a mile thick. It looked like nobody else had been here in years. Which wouldn't be a surprise. It was amazing how far one had to go to step outside Loki's sphere of influence.

"Excuse me?" Ella asked, clearing her throat. "Is Mr. Xi in, please?"

The old woman looked up, her eyes expressionless. She waited a few moments, then held out her hand. *A bribe.* It figured. It was almost funny, in a way. Ella rolled her eyes and pulled a twenty out of her purse.

The woman snatched the crumpled bill and shoved it into the pocket of her dress. Then she motioned for Ella to come behind the counter, pushing aside a dirty striped curtain hanging in the doorway and leading her through to a back room with a staircase. *Jesus.* They should really hire a cleaning person. Ella followed her up the dangerously narrow flight of stairs. It dissolved into darkness. There was no handrail. Ella felt her way along the wall as the stairs cracked underfoot, her hands touching decades of grease and grime.

Her lips pursed. She hadn't remembered *this* part, either. Then again, her mind had a knack for repressing memories of filth.

Like the secret hideaway she still maintained. The one she'd never told anyone about. The one she hadn't even thought about in almost five years. The one she vowed never to use. But there was no point in going there, either. Not even in her mind.

At the top of the stairs was an enormous iron door. Ella could barely make it out for the lack of light, but it looked a little like a bank vault. Hanging from the ceiling on a rusted chain was a small iron ball. The woman swung the ball against the door like a door knocker. After knocking six times she waited a moment. Then she knocked again.

Almost instantly there was a metallic sound of locks being turned, bolts sliding away. The dry hinges groaned as the door swung open, spilling a pool of cool blue light. A man in an embroidered tunic stood in the doorway, beckoning Ella to come forward.

"You are here to see Mr. Xi?" he asked, gently helping her inside the blue chamber. Ella nodded breathlessly, her eyes struggling to adjust to the light. Five-foot vases swam into view. Lacquered dragons. Antique tapestries of mountains threaded with silver. At least they kept *this* place clean. But were these pieces real? Ella wished she knew more about Chinese art. She wouldn't be surprised if these were just cheap props, designed to give the impression of luxury.

"Your name, please?" the man in the tunic asked.

"Ella," she replied, not bothering to give an alias. There was no point. Loki would figure her out eventually. He always did. "Ella Niven."

The man nodded, then led her down a passage to another darkened doorway. It was opened just the slightest bit. He turned and clasped his hands neatly together. "Mr. Xi?" he asked into the crack. "May I present to you Ella Niven?"

Ella bit her lip to keep from sneering. There was something so *absurd* about this whole ritual. Why couldn't she just talk to the man and get it over with?

After a few moments of silence a gravelly voice answered, "Yes, you may."

The man in the tunic motioned for Ella to step inside. She blinked, frowning, as she pushed open the door. The room was like a dark blue box drained of light—except for a slender spotlight that illuminated a single empty chair in front of a long, sleek table. Behind a Chinese screen at the far wall she could see the hulking outlines of six bodyguards standing at attention. The tiny red bulbs of surveillance cameras blinked in each corner.

"Sit down, Ella Niven," commanded the gravelly voice. It, too, came from behind the screen.

She took a seat in the empty chair, swallowing. She blinked in the harsh glare of the light. She could barely see a thing. Her heartbeat quickened. These rituals might be trite and annoying, but she had to admit it: They were effective. They instilled fear in a potential client. Ella knew that she wouldn't be able to turn back even if she wanted to. No doubt all six of those men were as highly trained as she was. . . .

A tiny man in a fedora stepped out from behind

126

the screen and stood at the opposite end of the table, by the door. It was too dark to make out any of his features, but his frame was very small and thin for a man. If Ella didn't know any better, she might have thought this guy was actually a twelve-year-old boy. Strange . . . she had been here once in the past, many years ago, but she'd never actually seen Mr. Xi.

"Uh . . . thank you for agreeing to see me," Ella murmured, holding her shopping bag protectively in her lap.

"I recognize you," Mr. Xi stated. His voice was throaty and disturbing, especially coming from someone his size. "I know who you are."

Ella nodded, fighting to ignore the twinge of fear that shot down her spine. This man could be on the phone with Loki in an instant—and there would be nothing she could do to stop him. She figured it was best to just shut up.

"You would like to employ my services," he said. It wasn't a question; it was a statement of fact. There was an edge of undeniable authority in his tone. Much like Loki himself.

"Yes," Ella whispered. *Why the hell else would I be here, you—*

"Speak up, woman!"

"Yes," she repeated, wincing. "I would."

"My services will cost you one hundred fifty thousand dollars," he announced.

Ella knew that this would be the amount. Still, hearing it didn't fill her with joy. With numbed fingers she pulled a shoe box out of her shopping bag. She removed the lid and stared down at the crisp blocks of cash—taken out from the Bank of Liberia on Tenth Street less than an hour ago. The transfer had been a success. And now . . . well, it seemed such a shame to be spending half of the money she stole so soon after she had stolen it. But she was resolved to do this. She slid the box across the table.

Mr. Xi didn't touch the money. He barely looked at it. Instead he snapped his fingers. One of the bodyguards rushed out to the table and hurriedly counted the bills. Then he nodded toward Mr. Xi and retreated back behind the screen.

"Whose life are you buying?" Mr. Xi demanded.

The directness of the question caught Ella off guard. There really *was* no turning back. They were coconspirators now, talking plainly about a murder.

"Her . . . her name is Gaia—Gaia Moore," Ella stammered.

"What is her relationship to you?"

Ella hesitated. "She's . . . uh, my foster daughter," she murmured, looking down at the table. For some reason, saying the words out loud made her feel ashamed. But why should they? Gaia Moore had destroyed her life.

"I'll need a picture," the shadow said.

"Of course." Ella reached back into the Barney's bag and pulled out a manila envelope, then slid it across the table. Mr. Xi stepped forward and removed the snapshot. He stared at it for several uncomfortable moments. Ella shifted in her seat. For a second she even waited for him to gush about how beautiful Gaia looked— like every other nauseating person on earth did. But thankfully, he didn't say a word about it.

He tossed the photo back on the table. "How do you want to end this girl's life?" he asked.

She shrugged. "I don't care. Just as long as it happens soon. She's a martial arts expert, though. She could be a little hard to get to."

Mr. Xi laughed. "That won't be a problem. But you are certain that this is what you want?"

Ella didn't allow a moment's hesitation. "Yes. Absolutely."

"You are certain?" he repeated.

Didn't I just say I wanted to do it? Ella wondered, scowling. "I want her dead," she growled. "Is that enough to convince you?"

"There's no need for rudeness," he answered calmly. "I will take your contract. You may go now."

Ella didn't move. Did he think she was some sort of idiot? She blinked hard in the spotlight. "How do I know you're actually going to go through with it?" she asked. "I mean, how do I know that you're not just taking my money?"

Mr. Xi sighed. "Faith, Ella Niven," he muttered. "Good faith. If I give you my word, the job will be done."

Ella clenched her jaw. That wasn't exactly reassuring.

"You haven't changed your mind, have you?" he asked.

"No," Ella said quickly. "Of course not."

"Good," the shadow said. "Because we operate by a strict code here. Once the money has changed hands, there's no turning back."

TOSSING THE EMPTY CANDY BAR wrapper in the trash can, Gaia tiredly resumed her post in front **Sadomasochist** of the dim sum house several doors down from Mr. Chin's. The sun had nearly set. A bitter wind had settled over the street. The crowd of pedestrians had begun to thin out, ducking into doorways like squirrels burrowing into holes for the winter. Gaia shifted on her feet, rubbing the sides of her arms through her coat sleeves. Ella had been in there forever. And Gaia knew that Ella sure as hell wasn't buying an old TV.

No. Whatever was going on in that dusty time warp of a store somehow involved Gaia herself.

Maybe she should duck inside the restaurant to get warm. But then she might miss Ella. She turned her head to look at the tank filled with striped sea bass in the window, their opalescent bodies undulating in the water as they pressed their fish lips against the glass. She couldn't help but smile. It almost looked like they were blowing kisses at her. She puckered her lips and air kissed them back. It was funny . . . in a really, really sick way. Well, actually it wasn't funny at all. Her smile faded. Now that Sam was officially dead to her, this was the closest to making out that she was likely ever to get.

But the window did serve a purpose. By staring into it at a certain angle, she was able to use its reflection to get a good view of the street.

Rule number two of surveillance—make use of reflective surfaces. It was best never to look directly at anyone—but to use car doors, windows, whatever makeshift mirrors were available. The city was full of them; that was one good thing about New York. And this large fish tank full of striped bass was as good as any—

Wait a second.

Gaia's eyes narrowed. Reflected there in the glass, she could see a shadowy image crossing the nearly deserted street: a woman with a blond French twist. Gaia recognized that hair. Didn't she? She watched as the woman walked back and forth a few times, then stopped and looked around as if she were lost. As discreetly as she could, Gaia cast the woman a quick sidelong glance. Yup. The shoes, the tailored suit, the French twist, even the purse . . . Gaia had seen her earlier today. It was the woman she had helped at the restaurant, the one whose purse had been snatched, then dumped in the trash.

Weird. Gaia continued to pretend to gaze at the fish. There were seven million people on the island of Manhattan . . . yet she ran into this woman twice in the same day? What were the odds of that? She figured she had a pretty good chance of repeatedly rubbing elbows with struggling actors and street thugs—but seeing a member of the Park Avenue set, especially down here, was just a little too unlikely. . . .

Maybe the woman was a sadomasochist. Yeah. Maybe she had a thing for getting mugged. Gaia watched in mild amusement as the woman absently swung her rescued handbag. Why didn't she just pull out a map and tape a sign to her back that said I'm Lost? For a moment Gaia was half tempted to walk over to her and ask the woman if she needed directions.

But that was when Ella walked out of the store.

She'd ditched the Barney's shopping bag. Gaia turned back toward the puckering fish. Curiously, the blond woman had vanished. Just like that.

But then Gaia caught a glimpse of her. Right behind Ella. The woman had pulled out a cell phone and was headed in the same direction as Ella was . . . almost as if she suddenly knew exactly where she was going.

Almost as if she were *following* Ella.

Gaia's gaze remained fixed on the glass. She didn't move. Ella turned left at the next corner. Five seconds later the blond did, too. Then Ella crossed in front of a cab. So did the woman.

That was all Gaia needed to see. It was no coincidence that the woman had appeared twice in the same day. Coincidences like that just didn't happen. Not in New York City.

Three's a Charm

"I'M RIGHT BEHIND HER," PEARL whispered into her cell phone. "We're on Pell Street, heading north."

"Make sure no one sees you," Loki instructed. "And call me when you're done."

The line went dead.

Pearl jammed the phone into her pocket. The threat was clearly implied: *Get the job done or die.*

She'd brought this upon herself, though. She'd grown careless.

But she wouldn't fail this time. Not this time . . . and not ever again. Her fear of Loki served a positive purpose. It enhanced her focus. She would remember that.

Ella was just a few yards ahead, her dreadful dye job flapping in the cold winter wind. Now that Pearl thought about it, Ella *wasn't* as beautiful as she'd once thought. Smiling, Pearl picked up her pace, her heels clattering on the sidewalk. "Ella?" she called. "Ella? Is that you? Yoo-hoo . . . Ella!"

Ella paused, turning slowly on her heels.

That's a good girl, Pearl thought as she waved. *Now, stay put this time.*

God. Even in the shadowy half-light of the streetlamps, Pearl could see that Ella looked like hell. What had Loki's fallen angel done since lunch? Fallen into a sewer?

"Ella!" Pearl called again, her face a mask of feigned happiness and surprise.

"Pearl?" Ella's eyes narrowed, then she laughed . . . a little awkwardly. "Wow. Twice in one day. I'm starting to think you're stalking me."

Pearl tossed back her head in a throaty laugh. But

she knew she would have to act fast. She closed the gap between them. Ella was smart enough to be suspicious of such a coincidence; Pearl couldn't underestimate her.

"I know—what are the chances?" Pearl asked. She shook her head. "I met up with a Chinese art dealer. He was supposed to have some genuine Ming vases. All junk. So what are *you* doing in this part of town?"

Ella hesitated, glancing distractedly up and down the street. "I had a little business of my own to take care of," she muttered.

"I see." Pearl winked, trying to loosen up her target, to get her in that mood where her defenses were down. "Something a little *naughty*, I hope?"

"Uh . . . what?" Ella asked, clearly not listening.

Pearl quickly surveyed the area. The location was good, but not ideal. On the corner was a small Asian deli with an outdoor vegetable stand. An elderly man with bifocals was poking through a case of bok choy. Hardly a damaging witness, but Loki had been clear. No witnesses. Pearl had to get her off Pell Street. Again her eyes scanned the sidewalk.

There. Up ahead, maybe ten feet, a little alley. Perfect.

"So how did things go when I left the restaurant?" Pearl asked sweetly.

Ella shrugged. "It was a complete disaster. I really don't want to go into it."

A heavy silence fell between them. That was fine. Pearl didn't feel like making small talk, either. She clamped her fingers firmly around Ella's wrist. "Come over here," she said, pulling her roughly toward the black abyss of the alley. "I want to show you something."

A wry grin suddenly crossed Ella's sullen face. "Another little something you picked up at the Frederick's sale?"

Pearl grinned, easing Ella into the darkness. "Not quite."

ELLA WASN'T ABLE TO REGISTER what was happening. For a panicked instant she thought she might be having a heart attack. Pain had very suddenly exploded in the small of her back. The wind was knocked clean out of her. One second she was standing with Pearl; the next she was collapsing against a cement wall, gasping, desperate for oxygen. She clutched at her chest and raised her eyes.

Pearl was leaning over her. She was no longer smiling.

"Help me," Ella croaked. "I—"

There was a blur of motion. Instinctively Ella held up her hands and crouched into a defensive kung fu stance. But something struck her chin. Another flash of pain exploded through her. Ella's stunned mind reeled, frantically trying to make sense of the situation. The hot, metallic taste of blood ran in her mouth. Pearl was attacking her. Why?

"What are you doing?" she wheezed.

Pearl didn't answer. Ella caught a glimpse of her topaz eyes . . . cold and dead. Void of feeling. Panic bells went off in Ella's mind, but she couldn't move. Her limbs were like wet cement, quickly drying, freezing her in place. She couldn't breathe. Silently Pearl delivered another punch—this time to her rib cage. Ella doubled over in pain. A sickening ache rippled through her torso. She had to defend herself. . . .

Why are you doing this? Why did you turn on me? Who are you?

Dozens of thoughts danced frantically through Ella's skull. But she couldn't help but notice something peculiar: for all Pearl's strength, there was a surprising lack of anger in her fists. Almost a detachment. This wasn't personal.

And that made the attack all the more dangerous.

Summoning what little strength she had left, Ella snapped into action—delivering a karate chop to the left side of Pearl's face as the woman reared back to launch another blow. That would buy her a few seconds to regroup.

The surprise force of the hit sent Pearl stumbling in her high heels, her arms flailing to keep balance. Seeing another opportunity, Ella pounced immediately, lashing out with a quick side kick that sent Pearl sprawling to the garbage-strewn cement.

"Who sent you?" Ella gasped.

Pearl rolled over and jumped to her feet. "No one," she panted. With her hair in disarray and face bathed in sweat, with her clothes stained and dripping with trash, Pearl no longer looked like the seductive socialite. Hardly. She looked like a deranged killer. She *was* a deranged killer.

"Tell me," Ella hissed, circling Pearl in a combat stance.

The two danced around each other, like two burning suns in mutual orbit.

With a sudden jerk Pearl deftly swung her legs in a half-moon, sweeping Ella's feet from underneath her. For what seemed like an eternity, Ella felt herself flying helplessly through empty space. When the flight was over, the only sound Ella heard was that of her bones slamming against the pavement.

GAIA STOOD STILL AS A STATUE AT

No More Ella

the mouth of the alleyway, waiting to see if Ella would get up. So far, Ella's fingers were moving, but little else. Gaia blinked. She had no idea what she was feeling—other than utter bewilderment. Ella was getting her ass kicked. That was no small feat, either. Shouldn't Gaia be dancing around with joy? Watching this should have been the best show she'd seen all week.

But it was just too strange.

First this woman had stalked Ella . . . then it turned out they were friends . . . then just as quickly the woman turned into a vicious assailant. But who the hell *was* she? And why did she want to hurt Ella?

Now the woman was kneeling beside Ella's crumpled form and opening her purse, the one Gaia had rescued from the trash. Even in the shadows Gaia could see something glinting. It looked like a glass tube and a vial.

The woman stuck the vial on the tip of the tube and pushed on it.

Holy shit. It wasn't a tube at all. It was a medical syringe. With a three-inch needle. Gaia shot a quick glance down the deserted block. It was dead silent.

139

Ella groaned.

Gaia peered back into the alley. The woman was pushing Ella's head down against the pavement with one hand and pinning Ella's arm down with her knee. Gaia caught the briefest flash of Ella's eyes in the darkness. She could see the whites. There was terror there. Ella knew she was about to die.

Time seemed to split in half—like a fork in the road, one path racing toward the past, one racing toward the future. Gaia knew that this was a pivotal moment in her life. Her body hummed with the cold energy that came in place of fear. Ella had made Gaia's existence miserable. Ella had tried to kill her. Ella had stolen the one boy Gaia could ever love. So why didn't Ella's impending murder fill Gaia with a sense of satisfaction? How many times had she fantasized about killing the woman herself?

But she's never been a victim before, came the silent answer.

That was the difference. That was why Gaia couldn't feel pleasure. Besides, allowing Ella to die wouldn't do Gaia a damn bit of good. Nothing about Gaia's life would change. She would still leave town with Uncle Oliver. If she could ever find him . . .

"Hold still, dammit," the woman hissed.

Gaia could just turn and walk away. Easily.

And then no more Ella.

The needle seemed to hang in the air, suspended in time.

In a vision as clear as any reality, Gaia saw the needle puncture Ella's skin and drive deep into her carotid artery. She saw the sudden jolt of pain and fear before the life drained from those hateful green eyes.

But she also saw a thousand unresolved questions slipping away. She saw mysteries without answers. She saw shame in herself for not intervening on behalf of a victim who was clearly helpless, at least for the moment. . . .

Before she even realized what she was doing, Gaia pounced into the alley.

"*Hai!*"

Startled, the woman turned her head—just as Gaia's foot made contact with her wrist. The syringe went flying. It danced and flipped in the air, hitting the ground with a shatter.

"Hey!" the woman screamed, her face blazing red.

She lunged at Gaia like a mountain lion clawing at the throat of its prey. Caught off balance, Gaia suddenly found the woman's bony fingers around her neck, squeezing tighter and tighter.

Surprisingly, they were very strong. Gaia's windpipe was slowly being crushed. But her mind was clear.

Raising her arms high above her head, Gaia quickly rotated her body 180 degrees. Her arms, combined with the sudden jerking motion, made it impossible for the woman to maintain her grip. It was a pretty basic move, one her father had taught her at the beginning of her training. Breaking a choke hold was a fundamental technique in all martial arts.

With the woman behind her now, Gaia pulled back her arm and jabbed an elbow hard into her side. Then she snapped her arm up like a lever, smashing the back of her fist into the woman's forehead. The blow landed sharp and solid. Clearly disoriented and hurt, the woman staggered backward three steps. It was all the time Gaia needed. Energy pumped through her joints as she launched herself into the air. Spiraling, she delivered a powerful roundhouse kick, smashing the side of the woman's face.

The woman collapsed in an unconscious heap.

Gaia towered over her, panting.

She'd done it. She'd saved Ella.

But before she could ask herself why she had done this ridiculous thing, black dots swirled at the edges of her vision and the ground rushed up to meet her.

I'M BEING CRUSHED BY THE PERSON

I hate most.

Surrender

It would have been funny if it weren't so terrifying. Ella lay pinned against the ground, Gaia's heavy body sprawled on top of her. Strands of Gaia's blond hair lay across Ella's cheek. The girl must be unconscious. Or dead. Ella stared helplessly at the gray sky. Pain pooled in her left shoulder blade. Had Pearl managed to stick the needle into Gaia as Gaia was finishing her off? Was that why—

"Are you all right?" Gaia groaned.

Ella blinked. "What?"

Moaning, Gaia rolled off her and sat up straight. "I said, are you all right?"

Ella couldn't answer. The question was absurd.

"You're the one who fell down," she finally mumbled. She swallowed, meeting Gaia's cold gaze.

Neither of them spoke.

Ella's eyes flashed to Pearl, then back to Gaia. Now that she thought about it, given the choice between being killed by Gaia or a needle, Ella would have picked the needle any day.

"Why did you come in here?" she whispered shakily. "To finish me off yourself?"

Gaia shook her head.

Ella's stare hardened. "Then why? Why did you do it? Why did you save me?"

143

"Because I want you to answer some questions," Gaia said simply. "And because you were in trouble." Her face darkened. "But believe me, if you were the one with the syringe, you'd be out cold right now yourself."

Ella didn't know what to say. She didn't even really know what Gaia was talking about. All she knew was that nobody had ever risked their life for her. Not even Loki.

Gaia was the first.

Gaia had appeared out of nowhere. *Gaia* had stepped right in and saved her. Ella turned her head away and bit her teeth deeply into her lower lip to keep the tears at bay. Shame and confusion flooded every cell in her being. She had underestimated Gaia's character. She had underestimated everything about her—

A muffled ringing noise interrupted her thoughts.

She looked at Gaia again.

"What is that?" Gaia whispered.

Ella's gaze flashed to Pearl's purse. Without thinking, she snatched up the purse and fumbled for Pearl's cell phone, then clicked the answer button. Whoever was calling Pearl might also know why Pearl had been sent to kill her. Ella didn't say a word. She simply held the phone to her ear. Gaia stared at her.

"Is she dead yet?" an icy voice demanded.

Loki. Ella's heart caught in her throat. Pearl worked for *him.* She should have known. . . . In a way, she supposed she always *had* known. But that didn't make the revelation any less terrifying. She hung up quickly, the phone tumbling out of her hands.

"What's going on here?" Gaia whispered.

"That was Loki," Ella gasped. "He was the one who sent . . ." Terror prevented her from finishing her thought.

Confusion clouded Gaia's eyes. "Loki?"

Ella slumped against the light post. He couldn't have known about the missing money so soon. The world seemed tilted, turned, inside out. Everything was backward. Loki was trying to kill her. Pearl was the assassin. Allies were enemies, and enemies were . . . Ella blinked hard several times to make the world right again.

But nothing changed. Gaia was still sitting beside her. Gaia had still saved her life.

NEVER IN GAIA'S WILDEST IMAGININGS

Stranger than Fiction

could she have imagined *this*: that she'd be helping Ella to her feet and dragging her away from the scene of an attempted murder. But her months of living in New York should have taught her something by now.

Never be surprised. Never be off guard. Never be close-minded. Reality was always stranger than fiction. Always.

They left Pearl unconscious in the alley and began walking—aimlessly, through the cold Chinatown night. Neither of them said a word. Their footsteps reminded Gaia of the ticking of two out-of-sync clocks. They marked the passage of time into an uncertain future. And with each second Gaia grew more impatient.

"Tell me what's going on," she demanded.

After several more steps Ella finally exhaled. "I don't even know where to begin," she stated.

"How about by telling me who you are."

Ella nodded, her head down. Gaia couldn't help but feel a wave of pity. Ella looked almost like a whipped dog; all the fight had drained from her. She was an empty shell. She was pathetic, lost, confused.

Much like Gaia herself.

"I've been Loki's partner for years now," she said.

Loki. There was that name again. Who was Loki? And why did Ella talk about him as if Gaia was supposed to know who he was? She'd never heard of *anyone* named after the Norse god of the underworld. The last time she'd even thought about Norse mythology was as a child, when her father had made her read a book about ancient religions. . . .

"He assigned me to you," Ella continued. "I mean,

the reason I married George was so I could keep an eye on you. Of course, George doesn't know anything about this—"

"Hang on a second," Gaia interrupted. She shook her head, trying to get her bearings straight. It was as if Ella were talking in some foreign language she didn't understand. "Why would Loki want you to keep an eye on me?"

Ella shrugged. "He wanted me to protect you because he couldn't do it himself."

Gaia froze in her tracks. For a moment she was almost tempted to laugh. "You were supposed to protect me? Then what the hell was up with the gun? The shooting? The attack—"

"Shhh." Ella's face grew serious. She glanced warily down the street. "That's why he's after me now. Because I tried to kill you. He . . . he cares about you." Her downcast eyes fell to the sidewalk. "He loves you more than anything. But his job . . . see, his job prevented him from making contact with you before now. . . ."

Suddenly everything fell into place.

Blood turned to ice in Gaia's veins. She felt like she'd been standing at the edge of a vast precipice for *years*, always looking down . . . and Ella had just shoved her over the edge. *His job.* Only one kind of job could have prevented somebody with a name like "Loki" from seeing her. Someone with a job that required an alias. A code name.

Someone like her father.

One of my greatest fears is that
someone will attempt to tell my
daughter why I left her. The reasons
are complicated and involved and can
be understood only by someone who
has actually lived through it.

I'm afraid that if Gaia hears
about it from someone other than
myself, she'll get the wrong impression. There are important parts of
the story that will invariably be
left out—like how much I love my
daughter, how thoughts of her con-
sume my every waking hour, how I
write letters to her only to file
them away because they cannot be
sent. Only I can express to her the
ache in my heart at having to leave
her alone. Or the pain I feel on her
birthday when I can't call or even
send a card.

If Gaia doesn't know any of these
things, if she doesn't have the complete story, then I'm afraid she could
get hurt from the misunderstanding.
I'm afraid I could lose her.

That's why I have to find a
way to tell her myself.

TOM

But things were different now. Much different. The **contract** hunters were the hunted.

ELLA KNEW THAT GAIA DIDN'T
believe a word of this.
Then again, Ella never
really *expected* Gaia to
believe her. But there
was something new
in Gaia's eyes now . . .
something Ella had

A Dangerous Place

never seen before. Was it curiosity? Anxiety? Fear? Any
of those emotions would have made sense. They were
all fitting when it came to Loki.

"Tell me about him," Gaia said.

For a moment Ella just stared at her.
**Discussing Loki's life was dangerous
territory.** The more you knew, the more jeopardy you were in. Of course, Loki would never harm
Gaia. That was the one certainty. "What do you want
to know?" she asked.

"Everything," Gaia stated. As if to prove her
point, she sat down on the curb. Ella hesitated. Her
eyes roved the street. There was a very good chance
that Loki was already coming after her. They
should get somewhere . . . somewhere safe. Away
from Chinatown. Her gaze came to rest on a large
window display. There were carvings and vases and
a huge tapestry of a mountain landscape, woven
with silver thread. Just like the one she had seen at
Mr. Xi's . . .

No. Mr. Xi.

Gaia had a contract out on her life. But Gaia had just saved Ella. There was no way. . . . Okay, yes, Ella *had* wanted her dead. But things were different now. Much different. The hunters were the hunted. Ella would need Gaia's help if she wanted to survive. And vice versa. Ella had to tell Mr. Xi the deal was off . . . if it wasn't already too late.

"There's something I have to take care of right away," Ella mumbled, her feet already in motion. A vague feeling of panic tingled at the base of her spine. "It's important."

"Hey!" Gaia shouted, leaping to her feet. "You can't just leave! You owe me some answers!"

Ella quickened her step. "It'll have to wait until later."

"Not later—*now*."

Ella stopped. "Look, Gaia—this is a dangerous place for you to be right now." Her voice was trembling. She stared at Gaia intensely, making it clear that defying her was not an option. "Meet me tonight at the building on the southeast corner of Avenue C and Eighth Street. We'll talk then—I promise."

"Why the hell should I believe you?" Gaia cried.

Ella didn't even attempt to argue. There was no point. "I can't answer that," she said. "Now get out of here."

Thankfully, Gaia turned and walked away.

153

ELLA WAS PANTING BY THE TIME

she burst through the door of Mr. Chin's. The old Chinese woman looked up slowly from her newspaper. Not even the faintest glimmer of recognition flashed across her weathered face.

Savage Swing

"Can I help you?" she asked.

"Mr. Xi," Ella gasped, struggling to catch her breath. Sweat poured down her forehead, even though it was freezing outside.

"Can I help you?" the woman repeated.

"I was here less than an hour ago," Ella stated, her brow furrowing in anger and confusion. "Take me upstairs."

The woman turned back to her paper. She didn't even blink.

Ella smacked her open palms on the wooden counter. "This is an emergency!" she shouted. "I need to see Mr. Xi now! Okay?"

Unruffled by Ella's outburst, the woman licked her gnarled thumb and delicately turned the page. Her lips silently formed the words as she read.

Shit, shit, shit . . .

"I've made a big mistake," Ella pleaded, on the verge of tears. Panic raged like a flash fire across her entire body. "A girl's life is in danger."

Still the woman kept reading.

Money. Of course. The woman needed a bribe. Ella gritted her teeth as she dove into her purse and pulled out a fifty. She slid the crisp bill across the counter.

The woman didn't even look away from her paper as she slipped the bill into her dress. "Mr. Xi is not here," she said.

Ella was half tempted to lunge across the counter and strangle this woman. "Well, where did he go? I have to talk to him immediately."

The old woman shrugged.

Fine. Ella was sick of playing games. Anyway, why was she even wasting her breath on the old hag when she already knew the way to Mr. Xi's lair herself? She stormed around the counter. With a look of alarm, the old woman jumped off her stool and threw herself in front of the curtained doorway, arms outstretched. Ella snorted, shoving the frail old woman aside as easily as if the woman were a straw mannequin. She headed for the stairs.

"You can't go up there!" the woman called, her Chinese accent melting away to perfect English. "Mr. Xi will be very upset!"

No problem. Ella was upset, too. She bounded up the rickety staircase in pitch blackness, praying that none of the dusty boards would suddenly buckle under her feet. She wouldn't get angry, though. No. She would just politely explain to Mr. Xi that she had resolved the conflict on her own, so there was no reason to go through with the contract. He could even keep the money for his trouble. A free $150,000. How could he possibly refuse?

In the darkness Ella spied the hanging iron ball that served as the door knocker. She even remembered the pattern—six hits, then silence. Then one more hit. Right. This was going to work out just *fine*.

Ella reached for the ball and swung it like a pendulum in the same deliberate fashion that the old lady had done. On the sixth hit she waited. Seconds ticked by. She knocked again—once more. Then she pressed her ear up to the cold metal. There were no sounds coming from the chambers on the other side of the door. Shouldn't the guy in the tunic have let her in by now?

Not good. She knew that fear and impatience were starting to get the best of her. But she couldn't help it. She tried again, slamming the ball harder and harder each round, the beats increasing in tempo. Still no one came.

"Answer the door!" she cried. "Just open the damn door!"

With a savage swing Ella smashed the ball so hard against the door, it broke from its rusted chain and lobbed down the staircase like a bowling ball. Her heart froze. She could hear the sound of decayed wood cracking in the darkness.

I've made some bad choices in my life. There's not a lot to be proud of.

Especially today.

I'm not trying to make excuses for what I've done, and I'm not looking for pity. All I ask is that before you judge me, bear this in mind:

Life doesn't always turn out the way you think it will.

When I was growing up in Connecticut, I dreamed of becoming a photographer. I wanted a husband I was passionate for, a couple of adorable kids, an apartment in the city, and a weekend house in the country. I didn't expect my life to be perfect, but I thought it would at least be comfortable. Normal.

Then one Saturday, when I was sixteen, I took the train into the city by myself to see the Annie Leibowitz exhibit at MOMA. Loki was there. He was the most charming, sophisticated man I had ever met. He asked me what I thought of the photographs. I couldn't believe he actually noticed me, actually saw me, when so many of the adults I knew only looked *through* me. At the time I was incredibly flattered by the attention. I thought he recognized something special.

Looking back, I now know that the only thing Loki recognized was my innocence. My willingness to trust. My vulnerability.

I won't pretend that I was so brainwashed by Loki that I didn't know the nature of his business dealings. It was obvious that what he was doing was dangerous, wrong, illegal, immoral . . . bad.

What *we* were doing.

But badness has a way of sneaking up on you. You tell a little lie or three—it's not so bad after a while. You skim a little money off the top from a rich terrorist—he wouldn't miss the money, anyway. The next thing you know you're taking out a contract on someone's life and you can almost justify it to yourself.

What I want to know is this: Is it just as easy to be good?

If I do something small, like smiling at some stranger on the street, can I eventually do something big, like helping orphaned kids? Or feeding the homeless?

Or leading an honest life?

Just once I want to do something noble.

Something I'm proud of.

Okay.

So this is what I know so far.

My dad's code name is Loki. For some reason he's in hiding, but he's been keeping tabs on me over the years to protect me. Ella's been working for him, and for some reason now he wants to kill her.

The way I figure it, there's two ways you can look at these facts:

A. Ella's lying through her teeth, and everything she's said so far is just a bunch of bull-shit, or

B. Ella's telling the truth.

If I went with my deep-down, basic-instinct, primal gut reaction, I'd pick A.

But here's the problem.

Let's just say for argument's sake that the answer is B and my dad really has been trying to watch over me all this time. Ella said he wanted to protect me. She also said that he wanted to kill her. If that's the case,

then wouldn't he want her dead
because she was probably trying
to hurt me? I mean, he wouldn't
do something like that unless
something big was at stake,
right? It makes sense. I keep
thinking back to that whole
incident in the park . . . the
one with Ella pointing a gun to
my head. My dad was there to
stop her, wasn't he?

So I guess that means if I
believe B, Ella unwittingly
incriminated herself. And if I
believe A, she's a liar just like
Sam.

Either way, I can't trust her.

Freedom was terrifying.

uncharted

She'd been a

ground

slave

for too

long.

FOR A CHILLY WINTER NIGHT,

Washington Square Park was unusually crowded. Students were huddled together on benches. Even a few in-line skaters were

The Words

out. Sam was a little surprised, and not because of the weather. Didn't anybody care about the fact that several people had been *killed* here over the past few months? Apparently not. Apparently *he* didn't, either. Everybody in this city seemed to suffer from short-term memory loss.

And he was one of them.

He spied some of his old chess buddies out at the tables . . . but his heart sank as he saw that Gaia wasn't among them. Zolov, the ninety-year-old Ukranian. Mr. Haq, the cabdriver. Sam hurried up to them, jamming his hands in his overcoat pockets.

"You come to play game?" Zolov asked, moving his red Mighty Morphin Power Ranger good luck charm to the left side of the chessboard. His eyes never moved from the pieces. Nor did Mr. Haq's. They weren't being rude; they were simply immersed in the game. Sam could relate.

"No time to play today," Sam mumbled. "I'm looking for Gaia."

Zolov's bushy white eyebrows knitted together. "Who?"

It took Sam a minute to realize his mistake. He'd forgotten that Zolov made up his own name for Gaia because he couldn't remember her real one.

"Cindy, Zolov. I'm looking for Cindy."

"Ah. Yes. Ceendy." Zolov smiled. "She's a good geerl. Pretty, too."

"I know," Sam said, trying to betray his impatience. "Have you seen her?"

Zolov took a few moments to consider the question. "No. I haven't seen Ceendy in a long time," he finally answered.

Neither had Mr. Haq, apparently. Mr. Haq just shrugged, frowning at the chessboard. A headache pounded Sam's temples. Where the hell was she?

She'd cleared out of her house, so she wouldn't be there. Ed Fargo said he hadn't seen her since this morning. She hadn't told Ed where she was going, either. And Sam hadn't seen her at Krispy Kreme or Ozzie's Café or Gray's Papaya. It was scary. Gaia didn't often stray from her usual haunts. . . .

As far as he could figure out, there were only two possibilities:

Either they had been running circles around each other all afternoon.

Or she was gone for good.

Zolov suddenly looked up. "Ceendy's your girlfriend."

It was a statement, not a question. Sam's rib cage

165

tightened around him like a steel band. "I . . . I wish she was," he confessed.

"Ceendy loves you," Zolov said with an impish grin.

Sam smiled politely, even though part of him wanted to smash Zolov across the face in frustration. But it wasn't his fault. The old man was obviously confused. He might be a formidable chess master, but he knew nothing about love.

IT WAS WELL AFTER MIDNIGHT BY the time Gaia headed toward the small East Village neighborhood known as Alphabet City. The area got its name for the lettered avenues that ran through it—not for any whimsical, childish reasons, like Alphabet Soup. It was a neighborhood of crack houses and abandoned buildings, of crime and hustlers and drugs. Even Mary, one of the more adventurous people Gaia had ever known, had never ventured too deep into Alphabet City alone. Day or night.

It was a good thing Gaia was fearless. Right

now, fearlessness was a good thing. The threat of street thugs and crack fiends wasn't enough to turn Gaia away. Nor was the possibility of running headlong into another one of Ella's traps. And as much as Gaia wanted to believe that Ella was finally ready to come clean, she knew it was unlikely. This very well could be one big setup. After all, why would the stepmonster suddenly turn on a dime and start being nice?

Because I saved her life, Gaia reminded herself.

Right. That had to count for *something*.

Gaia kicked a broken beer bottle to the edge of the curb, where trash was overflowing from a long-neglected garbage can. The outlines of listless bodies slumped in doorways faded as Gaia headed east; fewer and fewer streetlights worked.

"*Sssssssss.*"

Wait. Was somebody hissing at her? She glanced into the street. Yup. A guy with a pathetic excuse for a mustache had rolled down the window of his beat-up Chrysler LeBaron. Gaia had to laugh. Among the city's population of Neanderthals, hissing was actually considered to be a compliment.

"What are you, a snake?" she asked him.

The guy wagged his tongue at her. "No, but I've got one I can show you. . . ."

An inventory of kung fu moves flashed through Gaia's mind, but ultimately this caveman wasn't worth her energy. Gaia kept walking. After a moment the car sped away, turning the corner with a screech. Maybe that was supposed to communicate the man's disappointment. How clever.

What would Ella be doing around here? Gaia wondered. She pictured Ella walking by, wearing one of those spandex headbands that barely passed for a miniskirt, getting mauled by every other guy on the street. Then again, knowing Ella's voracious taste in men, she probably liked that sort of thing.

At last Gaia made it to the southeast corner of Avenue C and Eighth Street.

So. Here she was. Even among all the burned-out buildings and abandoned tenements, this *had* to be the worst block in the neighborhood. It looked like a war zone. Every window was broken or boarded up. Every wall was scribbled with spray-painted graffiti. On the opposite corner was a building with police tape draped across the doorway, declaring it condemned.

This *had* to be a trap.

Gaia nodded to herself. Ella would have never set a high-heeled foot anywhere *near* this place. So she had to be hiding in the shadows somewhere, waiting to pounce. Fine. Gaia balled her fists. The old, electric tingle shot through her body. She would wait for the ambush. It was all she could do.

FROM THE FOYER OF THE ABANDONED

No Safety Net

apartment building, Ella waited. She could see the street corner clearly through a cutout in the plywood that boarded up the window— with its dented mailbox that had been partially uprooted from a bad parking job.

Maybe Gaia isn't going to come.

Why would she? It was ridiculous to expect that she would trust Ella enough to show up at such a seedy address. Ella wasn't sure she even *wanted* Gaia to show up. Yes, there was a lot that Gaia needed to know for her own sake. But that meant that Ella would have to own up to her own past and the part she played in Loki's schemes. It was difficult enough admitting the truth to herself, let alone the person she'd been trying to hurt . . . even kill.

Absently Ella chewed on her newly cut fingernails while she waited. Maybe, just maybe, opening up to Gaia would be liberating. Maybe she would even catch a glimpse of her former self, that hazy vapor of a person stuffed into the bottom of her mind . . . the person who had once determined her own destiny and made her own decisions, without interference from anyone else.

No. She was fooling herself. Freedom was terrifying. She'd been a slave for too long.

This was uncharted ground—like hurling through space without a safety net. This was choosing one path among an infinite number. It was trusting yourself when you weren't even sure that you *could* be trusted.

Ella sighed and pressed her face up to the open hole in the plywood. What if, in the end, she discovered that she didn't like the person she was? *Anything's better than who you are now,* Ella told herself. *You can always change. . . .*

There she was. Gaia stepped up on the curb. She looked around, with her hands squeezed into tight fists, as if she were unsure she had remembered the address correctly. As if she didn't trust Ella at all.

Poor thing, Ella thought in silence. *She has no idea her life is about to change forever.*

THE DOOR TO THE RUN-DOWN
apartment building creaked open. Gaia hesitated. This was it. The moment. But Ella was nowhere to be seen. A young woman in olive cargo pants and a white T-shirt stood in the doorway. . . .

Ella Sponge

"Hello, Gaia."

Gaia blinked. No. It was impossible. Long gone were the miniskirts and sequins. The layers of makeup had been chiseled off and the offensive red hair had been pulled back into a loose bun, revealing a much younger looking face. Even the hideous red talons Ella had glued to her fingernails had been ripped off. It was hard to believe there had actually been a *person* under the clown costume Ella had always worn.

But there she was . . . looking not so different from Gaia herself. It was beyond strange; it was *creepy*.

"I barely recognize you," Gaia stated.

Ella managed a sad smile. She held open the door, glancing out in the street. "Come in. We shouldn't be outside."

Well, if this was a trap, Ella was doing a damn good job. Gaia hesitantly followed her inside. The entrance smelled of must and mold. There were no lights on anywhere, only a trail of votive candles leading from the front door to the second-floor landing. A rat whisked by in the shadows. This place was like . . . what? A crash pad from some sixties movie? A house of junkies? If there was ever a place built to the exact inverse specifications of Ella's personality, this was it.

"Sorry, there's no electricity in here," Ella apologized,

handing Gaia her own candle to carry. "Or running water, either. It's a squat. The roof leaks, and sometimes plaster falls from the ceiling. But hey, what do you want for free?"

Gaia shook her head. "How did you . . . find out about this place?"

"As soon as I moved in with George, I knew I had to find a place where no one could find *me*," she answered. "Nobody who knows me would look for me in a crack house in Alphabet City. Right?"

She had a point there. Gaia's limbs felt sluggish and dull, as if she were moving through a dream. She had no idea what to make of any of this. Footsteps creaked across the floor above them. A tinny radio echoed in the stairwell.

"Do you stay here a lot?" Gaia asked.

"Are you kidding?" Ella laughed, leading her down the second-floor hallway, past several doors marked with their own letters, to a single door at the end of the hall. The paint on the door was mottled and chipped, and a faded letter *E* materialized in the flickering candlelight. "I like the high life, remember?"

Gaia didn't answer. She decided she'd simply listen, observe, *soak in*. She would be a sponge—a sponge that absorbed Ella . . . or whoever the hell Ella really was.

Ella pushed open the door and led Gaia inside. It

was a dingy studio apartment—hardly bigger than Gaia's bedroom on Perry Street. A small army cot was set up in the corner, next to a sickly yellow bureau with flower decals that looked like it had been rescued from a street curb. On the other side of the room were a small chrome table and mismatched wooden chairs and milk crates filled with papers and folders. Candles dripped slowly on every available surface. A cockroach scurried up the wall.

"Sorry I can't offer you anything," Ella joked.

"Right," Gaia said blankly. She took a seat at the table. She scanned the apartment for weapons—guns, carving knives, baseball bats—but didn't see anything remotely threatening.

Ella sat down across from her. Again Gaia was struck by how *different* she looked without all the makeup.

"So, is this totally shocking to you?" Ella asked.

I'd have to say that's the understatement of the century, Gaia thought. But she kept her comment to herself. Ella was still an opponent, an enemy.

"I know it must be strange to live with someone and think you know them, only to find out they're someone totally different," Ella stated in the silence.

Gaia clenched her jaw. "I never felt like I knew you at all."

173

Ella arched her eyebrows. "You formed certain opinions about me," she said. Her tone wasn't angry; it was just matter-of-fact.

"I thought you were a back-stabbing witch who couldn't be trusted," Gaia replied. Maybe if *she* opened up, Ella would be more inclined to open up, too. "And I always knew you were playing George for a sucker."

Ella just smiled sadly again. "Sometimes you had good reason to be mad at me," she answered. "But a lot of times, in the beginning, I interfered because you were in dangerous situations. And occasionally . . . I did feel bad about George. Not often, though."

Okay. Ella was being honest. Gaia supposed she could grudgingly respect her for that. On the other hand, it was pretty damn convenient to say that Ella felt bad about George *now*. In fact, this whole freaking setup was just a little *too* convenient. And a little too weird. Ella was suddenly a lost, homeless waif . . . out on the street. From the West Village to Alphabet City. In less than a day. No way. Gaia still couldn't believe it.

"You were trying to keep me safe, so you end up trying to kill me," she remarked flatly. "That makes total sense."

"No—at first I tried to protect you, but after a

while you started to get in the way of a lot of things."

Gaia laughed bitterly. "Like Sam?"

Ella nodded without so much as batting an eyelash. "Like Sam. You've got to understand something—Loki had me locked in a marriage with a man who was twenty-five years older than me. And Loki was ignoring me. I was looking for a way to feel young again."

Loki was ignoring you? Did that mean what Gaia thought it meant? A bitter taste formed in her mouth. Hearing vague hints about a possible sexual relationship between Ella and her father was about the *last* thing she wanted to deal with right now. The Sam issue was bad enough. She didn't want to talk about *any* of this. But she could feel herself slipping . . . as if she'd lost her footing on a rocky slope. She was beginning to lose control.

"You could have gone after anyone," Gaia found herself saying. "And you went after Sam—"

"What can I say? I was jealous of you." Ella swallowed. "That night we spent together—"

"I *really* don't want to hear about it," Gaia interrupted. She felt a sudden urge to bolt from this freakish little room, from this strange bizarro universe where nothing was as it seemed. Even the Perry Street Penitentiary was preferable to this.

"Look, Gaia, the whole thing with Sam was *my* fault," Ella insisted. "I followed him to a bar and went after him. He was bombed out of his mind. He had no idea who I was until he stopped by the house to see you a few days later."

A lump formed in Gaia's throat. This was too much. Too much . . .

"It was just one night, nothing more," Ella continued. "I wanted a real relationship with him, but Sam didn't seem to want anything to do with me—"

"What are you talking about?" Gaia found herself shrieking. "He sent you that e-mail to meet him at La Focaccia! I *saw* it!"

Ella shook her head. "It was a setup." Her voice grew strained. She looked like she was on the verge of crying. "That would explain why Pearl was at the restaurant. Think about it. I doubt Sam knew what was going on. He's in love with you, Gaia. That's what destroyed me. That's what tore me apart."

Okay, so I lied.

I said as long as I got a chance to tell Gaia that I love her, it doesn't matter if she goes on hating me for the rest of her life. But that's not true.

It does matter.

I don't want Gaia hating me at all. When she thinks of me, I don't want her to get all tense and agitated. I don't want the thought of me to bring her any stress or pain or discomfort.

But even worse than hate would be indifference.

I'd rather have her loathe me than feel nothing at all. If Gaia just wrote me off and shut me out of her mind—well, I just can't imagine a worse fate than being some microscopic void in the history of her life. Being totally forgotten.

What I want—at the bare minimum—is to be a small, perfect memory etched alongside some

of her most treasured memories, a piece of something
good for her to call on when
life got her down. And if I
can't at least give her that,
then my life will add up to
nothing.

The memories were like a thousand needles, pricking her all over at once: the **the** ransom notes, the bizarre **truth** demands, the chases. . . .

GAIA STARED AT ELLA . . . WAITING
for the punch line, waiting for the
devastating blow that would suddenly
end this sick game. But none came. A
piercing ache drove itself deep into
her very core.

The Horror

Sam is in love with me.

The words squeezed her heart.
Gaia wanted to believe it. She *had* to believe it.

"I . . . what are you saying?" Gaia asked weakly.

"Sam loves you," Ella repeated.

Without warning, Ella reached across the table and
put her hand on top of Gaia's.

"I'm sorry," she said.

Ella is touching me.

Touching. Not kicking, not scratching, not
yelling, just . . . touching. In all these months it was
the only maternal gesture Ella had ever made. And
some strange part of Gaia—a part she never knew
existed or at least hadn't felt in years—longed for
the hand to linger that way, to let herself be moth-
ered. But she tensed and pulled away. She didn't
want to go down this path. She wasn't quite ready to
forgive. Once more she was perched on that
precipice, overlooking that dark
chasm . . . and she knew she would be a
goner if she dove in. She needed to learn
more. About *everything*.

"So let's get back to *you*," Gaia forced herself to say. But she couldn't hide the emotion that clogged her voice. "Who are you?"

Ella leaned back in her chair. "I don't know," she said in a faraway voice. A wistful smile crossed her face, then vanished. "It's funny. Once . . . when I was your age, I was a photographer."

Whoops. Gaia tried not to grimace at the memory of those awful black-and-white photos hanging in the hallway at George's brownstone. With everything else about Ella turning out to be fake, it was a kind of a shame that *those* had been real.

"Here, I'll show you some of the stuff I did," Ella suggested. She jumped up and pulled a box of photographs out of a milk crate.

All right. This was beyond weird; it was embarrassing and awkward and just plain freaky. Maybe now would be a good time to leave.

But as soon as Ella removed the lid, Gaia found herself frozen in place.

Instead of saccharine snapshots of kittens and touristy pictures of skyscrapers, Ella's photographs were intimate color portraits of people on the street. An old woman tugging at the hem of her skirt outside a bakery. The flash of anger on a businessman's face as someone else stole his cab. A melting pot of strangers huddled together under a deli awning during a rainstorm.

181

In a way, *this* revelation was the most shocking of them all. Ella had actually once had a tal-ent—aside from kicking ass and ruining people's lives and seducing men. Incredible.

"These are amazing, Ella," Gaia whispered.

Ella shook her head wistfully. "Just before I married George, a gallery in SoHo was putting together a show for me. But Loki thought it was a bad idea for me to be too successful. He thought if I was in the spotlight, it might blow my cover with George." Her voice turned bitter. "Now I think it was because Loki's massive ego couldn't handle my success."

Gaia's eyes narrowed at the mention of her father's code name. Suddenly all the old venom and anger came flooding back. Not only had Ella lied to her all these years; so had *he*.

"You two must have been quite a pair," she spat.

Ella stared at her. "Loki is a dangerous man, Gaia."

"No shit." Gaia's anger turned to white-hot rage.

"He's using you," Ella went on. "You're nothing more than a commodity to him."

A fire seared Gaia's insides like a branding iron. So there it was. The truth. In plain English. Her father no longer loved her.

"I'm out of here," Gaia announced. She stood up so violently that the table nearly toppled over. "I don't think—"

"No, no," Ella interrupted. "Not until you hear the whole story. Then you can do whatever you want. I swear it. Look, remember a few months back, when Sam was kidnapped?"

Gaia hesitated. Silence engulfed the room. In the flickering light of the candle, Ella's pained face suddenly looked grotesque. A cockroach skittered across the wall.

"You know about that?" Gaia whispered.

"I was there," Ella said gently. "Loki made you jump through all of these hoops to test your loyalty."

What the—Gaia's mind spun. The memories were like a thousand needles, pricking her all over at once: the ransom notes, the bizarre demands, the chases. . . . There was the mysterious videotape that appeared on her doorstep that she had to play in class. Then the public humiliation of Ed. The kidnapper had also forced her to steal something of George's.

"My loyalty?" Gaia found herself asking. "To who?"

"Sam. He said it was a test to see how far you'd go to save the person that mattered most to you—"

"No, no, no." Gaia shook her head, her tangled blond locks cascading around her face. "I don't buy it. Sam could have told you about—"

"Well, then, what about your friend Mary Moss?"

The room spun. Gaia's legs turned to jelly. "How do you know about Mary?"

"Loki decided you two were getting too close," Ella said. "It bothered him."

Now Gaia had to laugh. This had degenerated into the theater of the absurd. This wasn't a human being Ella was describing; it was some kind of omnipotent, insane, vengeful god. "You're telling me he was behind that, too?" she cried. "No way."

"He tapped your phones and had you followed—"

"Mary was killed by her drug dealer," Gaia corrected, her voice growing louder.

"That's what he wanted you to believe." Ella paused. "You probably feel like you've been born under some dark cloud, that tragedy follows you everywhere. You're not cursed, Gaia. It's Loki."

Gaia couldn't move, even if she wanted to. The strange and hideous room had trapped her. It was an inferno, one of the circles of hell; she was certain there would be no escape. "He kidnapped Sam and killed Mary because of me?" she asked hoarsely.

Slowly Ella nodded. "He was afraid you'd find out the truth about your past."

Her body went slack, as if she had finally surrendered. "And what is the truth?"

Ella took a long, deep breath. "Loki killed your mother."

A nuclear bomb detonated inside Gaia's head. The shock wave blasted through every cell of her body, driving her to the brink of a meltdown. Time gapped and seconds slipped into a black hole, spinning her back to that terrible night when she was twelve years old.

My father killed my mother. . . .

What Gaia remembered most was the snow. The way it fell soundlessly in a great silent wall of white. They were at their home in the mountains. Her mother was in the kitchen, and her father was setting up the chessboard. A fire blazed in the fireplace.

It was the last happy moment of Gaia's life.

Then came the twang. The mysterious, tiny sound from the kitchen. The one Gaia hardly noticed at all but that filled her father with panic, shoving her under the table for cover. He drew his gun. Shots were fired.

My father killed my mother. . . .

When it was all over, Gaia found her mom lying in a pool of blood.

The rest of the memory came in fragments. The ambulance. The night spent in the waiting room. Her father hugging her and walking down the hall. Then never coming back. In piecing together the events of that night, Gaia had come up with her own theory to explain the confusing events. There had been an intruder—either a burglar or a criminal her father had been tracking as a member of the CIA—and her father was simply protecting his family. And her mother got caught in the cross fire.

There was something fundamentally unsatisfying with her theory, something that didn't quite fit into place. First of all, Gaia had never actually seen *or* heard the intruder. And second, it still didn't explain why her father ran off. Disappeared.

Then there was Ella's version.

If Gaia's father killed her mother, then there had been no intruder to begin with. And it explained his disappearance. He had fled to avoid prison. He had fled to avoid facing his daughter after that horrible deed....

It all made sense now.

My father killed my mother.

Suddenly she found she was no longer standing. She was curled up into a tight little ball, her knees pressed against her mouth, shivering. Tears poured down her cheeks. Every fiber of her being felt like it was slowly being torn apart.

And Ella was right beside her. But Gaia was too tired to fight her off. Even postcombat exhaustion was nothing compared to what she felt now.

"I'm so sorry, Gaia," Ella whispered, stroking her hair. "I'm so sorry...."

Gaia was a little girl again. Twelve years old. Just like on that fateful night. All of her strength and badass abilities had trickled between the musty floorboards of this slum. She hugged her knees tight, hoping that if she made herself small enough, she might just disappear. "Why did he do it?"

"I don't know. He won't talk about it."

"I want to see him—"

"You can't," Ella said. "It's too dangerous for you."

"I have to," Gaia persisted. "I want to hear it from him."

For a long while Ella was silent. She wasn't even breathing. Finally she sighed. "Well, then I'm going with you. I owe you that much."

THE PHONE HAD NOT RUNG FOR HOURS.

Another Matter

Loki grabbed his cell phone and hurled it at one of the walls of his Upper West Side apartment. Bits of electronics and plastic rained down on the hardwood floor. Pearl wasn't going to call. That meant only one thing—Ella was still on the loose.

How she managed to survive this long was hardly a mystery. It wasn't that Ella had been too clever; it was that Pearl had blown her chance at every turn. Ella should've been the easiest of targets—hardly a challenge. She had been brilliant at following orders. Then again, so was his Doberman. There was a vast difference between doing what you're told and thinking for yourself. And Ella didn't have the brains to think her way out of a cardboard box.

It was Gaia who had saved her. That was the only explanation—

There was a knock at the door.

"Come in," Loki barked.

A squat man with an utterly unremarkable face and thick chest walked through the door. He was wearing a leather jacket. It was Bernard—or BFF, as Loki had always referred to him. One of the few Loki could still trust. Absolutely.

"We received a report that Ella has been spotted in the East Village," he stated. "Shall I give orders for Pearl to be executed?"

"Yes. You may go."

Bernard hesitated. "There's another matter that has been brought to our attention...."

One dark eyebrow arched suspiciously. Loki didn't like surprises. "Concerning...?"

"One of the Cayman Island accounts. Apparently three hundred thousand has been transferred to a bank in Africa."

Loki turned to keep his angry, balled fists hidden from Bernard's view. "Do you have the number?"

"According to our information, the account belongs to Ella Niven."

"I understand." Loki kept his voice and manner as cool as steel; meanwhile, his blood was boiling with rage.

"Is there anything you'd like me to do?" Bernard asked.

"No," Loki said, gritting his teeth. "This time I'm going to have to take care of it myself."

GAIA WAS AWOKEN BY A GENTLE

Safe

nudge on her shoulder. She opened her eyes to find Ella standing over her with a paper takeout cup of coffee. There was no brief moment of confusion as she woke up, no sudden rush of the events that had been gently wiped away by sleep. No. She didn't even know how long she had dozed. An hour, maybe less. And her nap had been plagued by awful, formless nightmares.

She sat up in the cot and rubbed her eyes, then took the coffee.

"We have a lot to do," Ella said, taking a seat at the foot of the cot. "But I'm glad you fell asleep. You needed the rest. Anyway, I want you to check this out."

She pulled a shoe box from underneath the cot and dropped it in Gaia's lap.

"Another box of pictures?" Gaia asked.

Ella shook her head. "Open it."

Carefully Gaia set the coffee aside and pulled off the top of the box. Inside were stacks and stacks of crisp hundred-dollar bills.

"How much is it?" Gaia asked, thumbing through the box.

"A hundred and fifty grand."

Gaia's stomach turned. "You didn't steal this from George—"

"No," Ella interrupted. "It's Loki's. I mean, it's ours now. When it's all over with him, I'm going to give you half."

Gaia swallowed hard. She couldn't help but think about those little twerps at the Union Square farmers' market, sticking their greedy little hands in the old man's guitar case for a couple of packs of Pokémon cards. Weren't she and Ella just as bad? Maybe it was best not to think too hard about it.

"So when do we go see him?" Gaia asked.

Ella's pale lips twitched. "You don't go see Loki," she said. "Loki comes to you. He's always moving around, changing his address and phone numbers. We'll have to draw him out. He's got so many spies around the city that all we have to do is stand in one spot long enough and he'll come for us."

Gaia frowned. "How do you know he will?"

"Because we've got his money," Ella said with a humorless smile.

Already the adrenaline was beginning to throb in Gaia's veins. She was still aching from the wounds of learning the truth about her father, but she shoved the hurt aside to wallow in a sea of unmitigated hatred. She would not be weak in front of the man who had single-handedly destroyed her life. She would not soften or break down. Gaia knew that the only way she was going to survive the confrontation was to turn her heart into a block of ice.

"Let's wait for him in Washington Square Park," Gaia said. She needed to meet him on her own turf. The home field advantage. Besides, it was late—the dead of night. Her favorite time to be out and about.

Ella nodded. "Just give me five minutes to find a place to hide this," she said, closing the lid on the money box. "It's not safe to leave it hanging around here."

As she waited for Ella to return, Gaia slowly sipped her coffee, thinking of all the things she was finally going to get to say to her father.

My world is collapsing once again.

I look back at that twelve-year-old, in the snapshot of me with my parents, and think about how naive she was, believing that nothing bad could ever happen to her. And now I look back at myself over the past five years and realize I was still just as naive—hating my father but never questioning his innocence. I thought my life was as bad as it could possibly get.

And then . . .

That image of my father and mother together, and our supposedly blissful life before the murder, was what I've held on to. I've clung to it the way a drowning person clings to a life raft. Sometimes it's the only thing that kept me breathing. But I see now that I was holding on to a lie. My parents couldn't have been in love if my father murdered her. Things couldn't have been as blissful as I imagined

them. My father certainly isn't
the man I thought he was. Ella told
me so much, and yet I feel like I
know even less.

I don't know who my parents
were.

I don't know who my father
was.

I don't know who I am.
I don't know anything at all.
But I'm going to find out.

But then she saw
the blood. It
had poured into
a thick black
pool around her
head, **sacrifice**
almost like a
halo. It was
more blood than
anyone could
stand to lose.

WASHINGTON SQUARE PARK WAS
utterly deserted. No freaks. No
druggies. No rapists. Gaia was
always amazed at how peaceful the park
looked when it was empty. It had been

Allies

hours since the hot dog vendors had closed their
umbrellas and pushed their gleaming metal carts
home. The last chess match of the day had ended
with the evening light, and now the tables stood
empty. By now most NYU students were safe in bed.
Sam included.

Gaia sat beside Ella on the edge of the large fountain in the center of the park, drained of its water.
There was nothing to do but wait. Wait for Loki to
show up. If he even *would*.

But Ella seemed certain of it.

"Are you scared?" Gaia asked. The information would be helpful to her, a way to gauge the
situation.

"Yeah," Ella admitted quietly. "I'm terrified. How
about you?"

Gaia shook her head. "I'm never afraid."

Ella laughed anxiously, peering down a pathway
into the shadowy, skeletal mass of trees. "I almost
believe you," she said.

"I'm serious," Gaia said. "I was born without the
gene that makes you scared of things." The words just
sort of fell out of her mouth. But it was a first. It was

196

the first time she'd admitted her *condition* to someone outside her family.

But Ella didn't even seem to hear her. She slid off the concrete wall and began pacing around, unable to keep still.

"Have you figured out yet what you're going to do with your half of the money?" Gaia asked.

Ella shook her head. "Maybe I'll go out west." In the dim lamplight her face was deathly pale—like ivory. Or bone. "Maybe I'll settle down and try to remember what it's like to be a photographer."

"Sounds nice," Gaia said, even though she knew Ella was lying. The shakiness in her voice betrayed everything. Ella didn't believe she was going to make it out of this park alive. Not that Gaia could blame her. It was best just to keep talking, to keep Ella's mind off her terror. "Do you need a roommate?" Gaia joked.

Ella laughed. "You have to fix things with Sam."

A gust of wind blew. Gaia shivered. "Sam and I were never a couple to begin with. There's nothing to fix."

"Don't lie to me, Gaia," Ella said, but her tone was very gentle. "You two have been dancing around each other for so long, but neither one of you has made an attempt to be honest with how you feel. That's why it was so easy for things to come between the two of you. You let it."

Gaia couldn't believe this. One day Ella was shooting at her; the next day she was giving her advice about the boy she'd stolen from her. But Gaia was willing to accept it. There seemed to be a kernel of truth to what Ella was saying. And maybe Gaia hadn't been a hundred percent honest about her *own* feelings. She had just kept waiting for him instead of taking the initiative herself.

Next time, Gaia vowed, *it'll be different.*

She cringed at the thought of all the rotten things she had said at the restaurant. She had called him a liar. She had told him never to touch her again. The memory of it was like a dagger twisting in her chest. Then again, he *had* slept with Ella. But at least she understood the scenario a little better. . . .

It probably didn't matter, though. Gaia might have no experience with guys, but she knew all about rejection. Oh, yes. And after the way she'd acted, no one would be dumb enough to give her another chance.

"THIS IS THE FINAL CALL FOR THE Midtown Direct train to Dover, making the following stops. . . ."

Once again Sam trudged through the waiting room of Penn Station as the announcer

Perpetual Motion

rattled off the list of stops for the next departing train. He was beyond exhausted. He was in a strange, hallucinatory state that came only with sleep deprivation. The white fluorescent lights were all too bright. His vision was blurred. He had circled the main concourse more than a dozen times, asking Amtrak ticket agents if they had seen a tall, gorgeous, angry-looking blond at some point in the last twenty-four hours. Sam knew how ridiculous the question was—but he figured it was worth a shot. Anything was.

No one would give him an answer.

His stomach growled as he passed a pizza counter. The only money in his pocket was a handful of change. Cab rides to both JFK and LaGuardia airports had left him flat broke. Right now he didn't even have enough money to take the subway. He was going to have to walk the thirty blocks back to his dorm.

The strange thing was, he didn't even mind.

He was beyond caring about anything. He took the escalator up to the street level. Gaia was gone. She had to be. He had been all over the city since yesterday. He would have definitely run into her by now. Well, no . . . actually, that was ridiculous. The city was huge. He *had* to keep searching. His body was aching, hungry, and tired, his feet blistered and sore. And yet he continued the perpetual motion, his mind with a single purpose.

If Gaia was on this planet, Sam was going to find her.

ELLA HUGGED HER ARMS TO HER chest, trying to ward off the chill that was seeping deep into her bones. Loki would soon be descending upon them. By now he had no doubt learned about **Peace** the money, about her betrayal. She could see him now, in that beautiful apartment, pacing the floor like an animal out for blood.

It probably would have been smarter to run. But Gaia deserved the chance to confront the man who had systematically ruined her life—all for some twisted notion of love he believed he felt for the girl. Ella wasn't about to let her face him alone. In a way, Ella needed this confrontation as much as Gaia did. She had a few choice words of her own to put a final cap on their long-drawn-out saga. Ella had been with Loki long enough to know that the only way to be free of him was to destroy him.

"What if he doesn't come?" Gaia asked.

"Don't worry—he will."

The wind kicked up, swirling around the two of them. Something faint and delicate fell out of the sky, brushing as soft as a feather against her cheek. Then another. And another.

"It's snowing," Gaia whispered.

She held her hands up to the sky to catch the flakes. The faint glow of the city illuminated the edges of her golden hair, making her look as graceful and fragile as a porcelain doll. Ella could see in Gaia's face that for a moment there was no Loki, no Sam, no worries or plans. For a moment there was peace.

That's when she noticed the man in the black coat and ski mask coming toward them.

He's here.

Ella's heart clenched. This was it. She could tell that it was definitely Loki, just by the way he carried himself. He was tall and lean, and his strides were graceful, determined—unlike the hulking clods he usually sent out to do his dirty work. Ella's shallow breaths quickened in her throat. He wouldn't shoot her . . . at least not right away. Loki would want her to know whose debt she was paying.

Gaia turned her head away from the sky. Her arms immediately fell to her sides as her gaze zeroed in on the figure. So much for her moment of peace.

"That's him, isn't it?" she asked.

"Don't say anything just yet," Ella warned. "Let me talk to him first." Her legs were shaking, and her mouth was dry. Yet even though her body was betraying her, Ella had never felt more sure of herself. She knew she was doing the right thing.

"I'm glad to see you finally made it," Ella called out. "We have a lot to talk about. . . ." Her voice trailed off. Through the holes of the ski mask Ella saw a pair of cold black eyes staring past her. Loki didn't have black eyes. His eyes were blue.

"It's not him," Ella whispered to Gaia.

"What? Who is it, then?"

"I don't know," she said. "But it's not Loki."

Loki must have decided against making a personal appearance and opted to hire a professional instead. *How typical.* Ella's eyes smoldered. Even in death he rejected her. He didn't even think enough of her to say good-bye in person.

At last the dark figure came to a stop right in front of the fountain. Whoever he was, he was as tall and thick as a tree, with muscled arms and legs that were nearly triple the size of Ella's own. She knew there was no way she was going to be able to defend herself against him. He was simply too powerful and no doubt trained as well as she was. As she desperately struggled to brace herself against the edge of the fountain, her slippery fingers lost their grip. The assassin raised his thick arm across his chest. Seconds dragged on like hours as his arm swung out toward them. Ella's muscles tightened in anticipation of the inevitable blow. She held up her arms to shield her head and waited for what seemed like an eternity.

That's when the assassin backhanded Gaia across the face.

GAIA FELT LIKE HER HEAD HAD

Fists Like Bullets

just collided with a brick wall. What the hell had happened? Why was this guy coming after *her?* Wasn't Ella the target? There was no time to question this mysterious turn of events, however.

Never let your opponent catch you off guard. . . .

Her father's words resurfaced in her mind. Gaia had let her guard drop once, but she refused to let the hulking brute catch her a second time. There was no time to think about who this man was or why he was out to get her—the only thing she had on her mind was survival.

Immediately Gaia was on her feet, fists raised in defiance.

The man in the ski mask greeted her challenge by raising his right fist and striking out at her with his left. Gaia recognized the move immediately. It was straight out of the *Go Rin No Sho*. Not only was her opponent strong, but he clearly had years of martial arts training as well. Not that she'd expected anything less.

Gaia met his fist with a successful block. Her entire body was buzzing now with adrenaline, primed to match him move for move. Out of the corner of her eye Gaia saw Ella stand up.

"Get away from her!" Ella screamed. She lunged forward and delivered a forceful kick to the side of his knee. On a person of regular size and strength the move could easily cripple an opponent, but the man in the ski mask just looked at Ella as if she were an annoying little flea. He clamped his hand around her throat, his fingers nearly reaching around the circumference of it, then threw her against the cement rim of the fountain as if she were a rag doll.

Not good. Not good . . .

Ella was writhing in pain—but she was also struggling to get back up.

"Just stay down!" Gaia ordered.

The man in the mask thrust his powerful fist in Gaia's face, just barely grazing the tip of her nose. Instinctively Gaia grabbed his thick wrist with both hands and rammed the toe of her boot deep into his shin. It was like kicking a rock wall. He didn't even flinch. His fists flew at her like bullets. Right jab. Left. Left hook . . . Gaia's arms blocked every hit with exhausting speed, accelerating in velocity as he quickened his moves. There was no time to think, only to react. He drove her back and kept coming up on her, keeping her on the defensive. This was bad. Very, very bad . . .

Gaia leaped back several feet to gain distance between her and her opponent. As he charged at her, Gaia grabbed his wrist a second time and bent it, using his own strength against him to push back his fingers. The man in the mask grunted in pain. In a fraction of a second Gaia delivered a strong round-house kick to the neck that knocked him slightly off balance. He staggered a little while Gaia took another leap backward to gain some distance.

She stared deeply into his eyes.

Who are you? What's your connection to my father?

But even as the inevitable questions surfaced, the attacker regained his balance, then leaped in the air and executed a flawless front snap kick aimed right for her stomach. Gaia dodged the assault, then took after him. Sailing into the air, she launched into a flying side kick, focusing all of her power and energy into her legs at the center of his chest. The bottom of her boot had just barely connected when the man clamped his hands onto her foot, then twisted it. Her body followed the complete rotation, spinning her 360 degrees in the air.

She knew she had been defeated even before her head hit the pavement.

ELLA WATCHED FROM THE SAFETY

of the fountain, filled with a sense of horror and helplessness as Gaia's head hit the ground. Desperately she wanted to intervene, to help Gaia in any way she could, but her arm had been badly broken in the fall. Nausea and pain overcame her as she stared down at her lifeless arm, with its shard of gleaming white bone protruding from her broken skin. There was nothing she could do.

Gaia lay still. The assassin stood over her.

I can't take any more of this, Ella thought as she looked away. A steady stream of tears poured down her face. *Why would Loki want his niece dead?* Anguish shredded her insides as she thought about how insanely foolish she had been, taking all of her frustrations out on Gaia. It was *her* fault that her life had turned out badly. And all the time she had been blaming her foster daughter. They should have been friends. Partners. Allies instead of enemies—

Yes!

Miraculously Gaia leaped to her feet. Ella was amazed by her stamina, even though Gaia looked a little unsteady. She and the man circled each other, arms and legs flying in a tangled mass. The assassin moved with effortless grace, as if he had hardly broken a sweat, while Gaia fought fiercely, matching punch for punch, kick for kick.

Ella's heart throbbed with admiration. She had never seen anyone so brave in her entire life.

LUCKILY THE BLOW TO THE HEAD

Crash

disoriented Gaia for only a few seconds. The pain throbbed, but she was still able to fight. The pain also had the added benefit of enraging her.

The man in the ski mask came at Gaia with a knee strike. She turned, thrusting her elbow hard into his solar plexus. She was pure, pulsating adrenaline now, operating at full throttle. Her reaction times were instantaneous; the force of her kicks had doubled in strength. There was even a flicker of surprise in her opponent's eyes as she fought on. Every last cell in her body was running at peak performance.

But Gaia knew she couldn't last too much longer. She was going to run out of gas very soon.

Furiously Gaia smacked him with an elbow to the jaw. He rammed his heel into her sternum with a back kick. Gaia gasped in pain. He followed with another knee strike and a kidney punch. Gaia spun and struck at his neck with one, two, three hits. With concentrated force she drove the heel of her hand up into his nose, sending the towering man reeling, with blood soaking into his ski mask.

Gaia's stinging lungs devoured the air. Already the adrenaline rush was beginning to subside, and exhaustion was kicking in. She had only a few seconds left before collapse. The man's eyes flared with anger as he plowed toward her.

Just hang on . . . just for a few more seconds . . . , she told herself. Her vision was getting dimmer, and the sounds of Ella's crying were growing more distant. As he barreled toward her, Gaia planted her feet firmly on the ground. He thrust out his arm. As soon as he was within striking distance, Gaia reached out for it. Using his own weight and momentum, she turned with her back to him and leaned forward, flipping him over her shoulder. He landed with a heavy, certain thud.

Gaia's muscles quivered in rebellion, begging for rest.

She turned slowly, prepared to fully immobilize her opponent, when suddenly she felt a pair of large hands reaching for the collar of her coat. Before she knew it, he'd planted his feet on her stomach. Rocking backward, he threw her clear over his head.

As Gaia sailed through the air, the last thing she noticed was that the snow had stopped.

GAIA DIDN'T GET UP THIS TIME.

The Sum Total of a Life

And now that she was lying on the ground unconscious, Ella knew she was going to be next.

Clutching her broken arm with her good one, Ella wobbled to her knees. Slowly she inched backward, her nerves screaming at her the entire time, in a miserable effort to get away.

But the assassin wasn't interested in her.

Instead he remained standing over Gaia, staring down at her unmoving body. The man then opened his coat and pulled out a gun.

In a flash of horror Ella finally understood what was really going on.

This wasn't one of Loki's men. This guy worked for Mr. Xi. He was the assassin Ella had hired herself to kill Gaia.

And he was about to finish the job.

The full weight of shame came collapsing down on her now, burying her like in the rubble of an earthquake. Tears wrenched from the very depths of her soul and fell on her arms in heavy drops. So this was what her whole life had come to. Of all the things she could have done with it, this was its sum total.

Through the blur of tears she saw the assassin press the barrel of his gun to Gaia's forehead.

"Ella Niven sent me to kill you," he stated.

"Don't!" A strangled cry rose up from Ella's throat. Maybe there was still a chance to do something right. Something honorable. "Don't shoot her!"

The assassin put his finger on the trigger.

"There's been a mistake!" she sobbed. "I'm the one you want! She's Ella Niven! I'm Gaia Moore!"

His cold black eyes flashed from Gaia to Ella. Doubt flickered there, as though he didn't want to believe her. But then he took the gun off Gaia's head. Ella crawled forward and tilted her own head up toward him. The barrel felt cold against her skin.

210

Gaia will be all right now, Ella told herself as she squeezed her eyes shut. And that meant her own life hadn't been a waste. No. She'd salvaged it.

The man pulled the trigger.

RETURNING TO CONSCIOUSNESS WAS

Alone Again

usually like surfacing after a deep-sea dive, rising up out of the still, dark weightlessness and returning to a world of noise, light, and motion. But this time, as Gaia's limbs began to stir, there was a noticeable absence of movement around her. It was as if the whole world had been silenced.

Am I dead?

Maybe the man in the ski mask had gotten the best of her, and now her life was over. But if that were so, then why did she feel pain? Now just wasn't the best time for things to end. She still needed to confront her father. And then there was Sam. There was so much unfinished business with him, some things she needed to say. And what about Ella? She seemed to have everything sorted out, but didn't she still need Gaia—

211

A sharp twinge wrenched Gaia's back.

She rolled onto her side. As her nerve endings slowly returned to their normal state, she began feeling the pull of gravity again and the rough, weathered edges of the pavement underneath her body. The muffled *whoosh* of distant cabs hummed in her ears. Streetlamps glowed orange from behind her eyelids. Gaia was still earthbound.

With a heavy groan she opened her eyes. For a moment she expected another round of blows.

But nothing happened. The man in the mask seemed to have disappeared. He could have easily finished her off if he had wanted to, but for some reason, she was spared.

Like a camera coming into focus, Gaia's eyesight sharpened as blurry forms took on crisp edges. There was a black swatch rising out of the ground that morphed into the leg of a park bench. A broad patch of gray curving into the edge of the fountain. A blotch of pearly white molding itself into the form of a hand.

A hand.

Gaia propped herself up as her eyes followed the hand to a wrist. *He must've beat up Ella, too.* Her eyes continued to travel farther up the broken arm to the shoulder. Ella had been knocked out. A deep moan rattled in Gaia's chest as she willed herself upright. It could be bad. She was going to have to bring Ella to the emergency room.

But then she saw the blood. It had poured into a thick black pool around Ella's head, almost like a halo. It was more blood than anyone could stand to lose. And then there was the bullet hole. A clotted black circle in the middle of her forehead.

Ella was dead.

Gaia didn't have to be conscious when the scenario unfolded to know what had happened. No, the aftermath seemed to spell it out clearly. Ella had stepped in when the man was going to kill Gaia. She had sacrificed her own life to save Gaia's.

The assassin's words rang through Gaia's head: *"Ella Niven sent me to kill you."*

But somehow, it didn't even matter that Ella had sent him. That had been the old Ella: a lost, confused, and tortured soul. That had been before she and Gaia had reached an understanding. In the end, Ella had redeemed herself. She had been a true friend and ally after all.

Gaia collapsed beside Ella and rested her head on her lifeless shoulder as convulsive sobs rocked the very core of Gaia's soul. She was drowning in waves of gratitude for Ella's sacrifice and overwhelming grief for her loss. And shame. Just yesterday she had actually debated whether or not she was going to step in and help Ella while she was fighting for her life. And now, twelve hours later, a dark, black void was opening in Gaia's chest, right next to the spaces that her mother and Mary used to fill.

Now there was a new one, and it belonged to Ella.

IT WAS ALMOST MORNING.

As Sam walked through the small-scale Arc de Triomphe at the Fifth Avenue entrance of Washington Square Park, he could feel the darkness lifting. The black outlines of buildings against the sapphire sky began to take on color as the light of dawn slowly seeped across

Nice Dream

the city. The winds had come to a standstill, and the temperature had risen to humane levels. Weatherwise, it seemed like it was going to be a pretty nice day.

Sam's feet moved slowly, still refusing to bring him back to his dorm for some badly needed sleep. His head felt thick and heavy, fogged over, and hunger gnawed at him relentlessly. But he had no desire for sleep or food. The only thing in this world that he wanted was Gaia—and she was gone.

He wondered where she was right now, what she was doing. She was probably sleeping, like most normal people at this hour. He wished for her a deep, restful sleep . . . and maybe a few pleasant thoughts that included him.

That will never happen.

But wherever Gaia ended up in life, he wished the best for her. He wanted her to be happy and well taken care of, to be surrounded by people who loved her. He wanted her to feel secure. He would have gladly provided all of those things for her. But he couldn't. He could only pray that Gaia would find someone who could.

Sam's thoughts seemed to exist outside himself. His mind was moving in directions he hadn't imagined possible. He knew he'd meet someone else someday and maybe even settle down and get married—and he might even be content—but it would never be the same. No matter what life would bring him, he would always know that he had glimpsed perfection. . . . He had seen what love really could be. And once you'd had a taste of that and lost it, you could never be truly happy again.

So he trudged on, past the fountain. Maybe they'd meet up again someday, when they were old and widowed, when they had most of their lives behind them. By then Gaia would be ready to forgive him. And that old spark would still be there. And they could finally be together. Just like they were meant to be. They would spend the rest of their days laughing and feeding pigeons and playing chess. . . .

A fantasy. A nice pipe dream from the movies. But it was all he had.

GAIA RESTED HER HEAD ON ZOLOV'S

Tears chess table. Slowly energy pumped back into her tired limbs. Dawn was finally breaking, and soon the city would be stirring to life. Soon students would be shuffling off to classes, storefronts would raise their scrolling metal gates, cabs would be hailed and buses taken to offices all around Manhattan. But for the moment the streets were empty and still.

There was no greater isolation than feeling alone in a huge city before sunrise. It had a way of making you feel like the last person on earth.

In a way, Gaia wished she was.

If there were no one else, then there was no danger of losing someone ever again. If she was the only person left on the planet, Gaia would automatically know that she was destined to be alone for the rest of her life. And that was okay. Once you knew what you were up against, you could deal with it. It was the continual hope of getting close to someone that killed you.

A band of golden light rose up from behind the buildings that flanked the park. A deep sob wrenched itself loose from where Gaia had buried it and rose up to her throat. A few tears stung her eyes, and soon they flowed freely. Anguished cries shuddered through her body, dredging up years of pain and loneliness, anticipating the bleakness of years to come. There were tears lost for her mother and betrayal of her father. Sorrow for Mary. Confusion over an Ed she no longer recognized. Regrets for Ella. Anger over her messed-up life

And Sam. Sam Moon. The Boy That Never Happened...

There was so much to cry for, Gaia didn't think she'd ever be able to stop.

SAM WAS ABOUT TO TAKE A RIGHT

Mirage at the dog run and head back to his dorm, but at the last second he changed his mind. He decided to head to the chess tables instead. Maybe he was being a masochist by surrounding himself with places that reminded him of Gaia, but at the moment he needed something—*anything*—that could make him feel close to her.

The sun was finally in the sky, bathing the park in the orange-yellow glow of early morning sunlight. Morning was his favorite time, when the day was ripe with possibility. No matter what was going on in your life, morning had a way of giving you hope.

Sam walked on, through the children's playground toward the southwest corner of the park. He would've liked to have shared a morning like this with Gaia, just sitting quietly with her while watching the sun rise....

Stop it. Just stop it . . ., Sam scolded himself. *You can't go through the rest of your life dreaming of someone you'll never have. . . .*

And then, as if his mind were rebelling, Sam saw Gaia sitting there.

Where she always should have been.

She was sitting at Zolov's table, with her head resting in her arms, her beautiful hair sliding off the side of the table in a tangled blond waterfall. Her shoulders were shaking, as if she were crying.

Twenty-four hours without sleep, and this is what you're reduced to—hallucinations.

Sam blinked hard and shook his head, but when he opened his eyes again, she was still there, bathed in golden sunlight.

First on the agenda was to sleep. Then he'd check himself into the psych ward at St. Vincent's. But maybe, before anything else, he'd enjoy the mirage for just a little while longer.

GAIA TILTED HER DAMP FACE toward the sun, the bright light washing every tree and branch with gold. In the distance the figure of a man approached, crowned with

ginger-colored curls. Gaia's heart throbbed in her chest.

Sam. Sam. Sam . . .

She lifted her head off the table and wiped her eyes with the sleeve of her coat. She watched his strong arms swinging gently at his sides as he drew nearer. If this was a dream, then that was fine. Because she desperately wanted those arms around her, holding her, shutting out the rest of the world. Only those arms could provide solace. She gazed at his soft lips. She saw the raw pain of his heart reflected in those hazel eyes. At that moment she wanted, more than anything, to wash it away. Because it would take her own pain with it.

WHAT SAM SAW WAS NOT MADE UP

Connected

of dreamlike vapor but the rounded, three-dimensional contours of flesh and bone. Instead of floating or evaporating into an ethereal mist, she seemed to be obeying all laws of the physical world. This Gaia before him wasn't a ghost or a hallucination. She was for real.

Their gazes locked.

With blood rushing in his ears, Sam stood before

219

her. For a brief instant he reached out to touch her on the shoulder but hesitated at the last second. He held his hand suspended in the air, then let it drop by his side.

"Ella's dead," she whispered. "She's over by the fountain. . . ."

The words barely registered. Sam didn't know what to feel. He only knew he didn't want to look in the direction of the fountain or ask what had happened. He didn't want to contribute to Gaia's pain. Now was not the time for questions. It was time for explanations.

"Gaia, I just want to tell you that I'm sorry for everything—"

"It's all right, Sam."

"Please just listen," he begged. Before he even realized what he was doing, Sam was holding her firmly by the shoulders. This time she didn't curse at him or resist. This time she didn't pull away. She was rising up from the table. She was returning his embrace. Tenderly his finger grazed the long, graceful curve of her neck and slowly tilted up her chin so that she stared directly into his eyes.

"Gaia, I love you."

The Moment

GAIA FOUGHT TO SHUT OUT THE WORDS, to not let them seep in, but it was too late. They had worked their way inside her, filling the wounded cracks of her soul. She tried to tell herself that it couldn't be true or that it would only lead to heartbreak in the end, but her heart wouldn't allow it. And to her amazement, Gaia found herself pressing herself against Sam. Wrapping her arms around his neck. As though she knew exactly what to do. As though she had done this a thousand times before.

"I love you, too," she answered. The words felt strange on her tongue. But they were the right words, the ones she had longed to say.

Sam swallowed hard, his hazel eyes smiling down on her. His strong arms seemed to speak for him, tightening around her waist and holding her so close against him, it was almost as if he never would let go.

With timid fingers Gaia explored the line of Sam's jaw, the sensuous curve of his mouth. Slowly she withdrew her hand and pressed her lips to his. The heat of his touch flooded her senses. For a long, slow moment she stayed there, breathing in Sam's warmth.

Whatever had come between them in the past had been obliterated. The only thing that mattered now was that they were together.

So this is love, Gaia thought, losing herself in another blissful kiss.

It was like coming home.

Holed up here in this hospital room, I've had a lot of time to think about the past. I've had time to reflect on how I could have changed it. This is very dangerous for someone in my profession, but sometimes the mind works independently of the will—no matter how much training a person may have had.

I've come to realize that until the time I was a young adult, three separate forces conspired to make me into the person I am today. These forces molded me, and, in the process, they took the two people I love most.

The first was my mother. More specifically, it was her devout Roman Catholicism. She taught me that piety, above all, would save my life. And I believed her. She instilled in me a desire to serve something greater than myself. So by serving my country, by helping to rid the world of criminals and terrorists and extortionists of the lowest kind, I truly believed

I would be serving God. It sounds ridiculous to me now. Even worse, it sickens me. Because I know that all the while, I was just serving myself. I was patting myself on the back for all the terrible secrets I kept and all the horrors I witnessed. I was allowing myself to feel superior. I was a hypocrite.

Which leads me to the second force. My brother. My twin. Loki never had the same problem with hypocrisy that I did. He rejected my mother's faith from the start and decided that he would live his life according to one set of laws: his own. And in this cru-cial way, despite the countless number of lies he has told, he has always been a more honest person than I have ever been or ever will be—because he is honest with himself.

Understanding this about him made me an expert in my field. Few people are more dangerous than those who are completely at peace with their own motives and desires. I knew this about Loki intuitively, from the time we were children. His mind fascinated me, because it was so similar and yet completely alien . . .

In any event, the third force, which is in some ways the most powerful, is also the most difficult to define.

It is my loneliness. Or no . . . maybe that's the wrong word. It's my self-imposed solitude. I've always been an outsider, an observer. I've never truly *belonged* anywhere—which, as I understand it, is rare for a twin. But Loki and I were islands; besides, our family was never known for its intimacy. The only exception was that brief, blissful period when Katia, Gaia, and I were together. As one. And when that ended, I slipped back into my old skin. I wore the shell that keeps the rest of the world at bay.

And it has nearly destroyed me and everything I care about.

The protective solitude has kept me from interfering directly with Gaia's life over these past few months. Of course, this isn't what I've told myself. No, I justified my distance by the empty belief that I kept her safe from danger, that contact with me would have placed her life in jeopardy. I rationalized my own behavior to the point where I could only trail Gaia around like a voyeur. And was I helping her in any way? Was I protecting her? Somehow, she only slipped farther into Loki's orbit . . . into the plans he has for her. Plans that I can't even begin to imagine. That I won't allow myself to imagine.

But the period of solitude is over. I won't let the forces of my past control me any longer. I'm going to be the father I never was. Or I'm going to die in the process.

Nearly two decades of waiting are finally drawing to a close.

I never had you, Katia, but I will have our daughter.

Yes. *Our* daughter.

I no longer think of Gaia as having anything to do with Tom. Genetically, he and I are one and the same. That is all that matters. In areas of consciousness, of personality, of all the intangibles that go into making a human being's *individuality* . . . Gaia is far more my own than my twin's. I've studied her from afar; I've interacted with her on an intimate level; I've watched her transform from a lost little girl to a self-assured woman.

And she has passed the final test.

Ella is dead. Whatever delusions she may have suffered in the last moments of her life, whatever misguided attempts she may have made to give Gaia a sense of peace and closure, she will always represent one thing to that girl: Deceit. I will make sure of it. I *have* made sure of it. There is nothing left for Gaia here. It is time to make my final and decisive move—to take her away from this city, to take her away from her past . . . to reinvent her.

Katia, if you could only glimpse what I have in store for our precious daughter, it would change your life. Because Gaia is indeed far more special than either of us ever dreamed. She is the future. Not just my own. She is *everyone's* future.

The vision is nothing more than a sketch at this point, nothing more than a vague collection of ideas and plans. But it will become a reality. Once you tip a boulder over a cliff, it doesn't stop rolling. It gathers speed and momentum. It becomes a force unto itself, independent of that first light push.

All my life, Katia, I've dreamed of leaving a lasting legacy. I've dreamed of an accomplishment that will be remembered a thousand years hence. And I've never lacked the desire to make it happen. I've only lacked the right tool. But now . . .

No—it's too impersonal to refer to Gaia as a "tool." She defies description. You already know that, though. One day, my love, history might invent the means to categorize Gaia. But for now, no such term exists.

Only one possible obstacle stands in the way of Gaia and me. You know what it is, Katia. Rather, you know *who* it is. Only Tom could possibly interfere with us. He is resourceful, brilliant . . . but he has an Achilles' heel.

Himself.

He is too clouded by false emotion, too clouded by his own self-inflicted wounds. He is weak. His weakness will be his death.

And his death will mark the beginning of Gaia's new life. *Our* new life.

FEARLESS™

LET'S FACE IT, GAIA MAY HAVE BEEN
BORN WITHOUT THE FEAR GENE—BUT
YOU WEREN'T, AND TO BE A FLY FEMME
FATALE ON THE GO, YOU NEED A BAG OF
TRICKS! RIGHTING WRONGS AND
AVENGING EVIL IS A FULL-TIME GIG AND
A GIRL'S GOTTA BOUNCE AT A
MOMENT'S NOTICE.

TEST YOUR *FEARLESS* TRIVIA. YOU
COULD WIN A MESSENGER BAG
JAMMED WITH ALL THE STUFF YOU
NEED TO KEEP **YOU** MOBILE—FROM
LIPSTICK TO A LAPTOP, YOU WON'T
BELIEVE WHAT'S PACKED IN HERE!

CHECK OUT WWW.ALLOY.COM
FOR YOUR CHANCE TO WIN

FEARLESS™

OFFICIAL RULES FOR
"WIN A FEARLESS MESSENGER BAG AT ALLOY.COM"

NO PURCHASE NECESSARY.

ELIGIBILITY: Sweepstakes begins August 1, 2000 and ends September 30, 2000. Entrants must be 14 years or older as of August 1, 2000 and a legal U.S. resident to enter. Corporate entities are not eligible. Employees and the immediate family members of such employees (or people living in the same household) of Simon & Schuster, Inc., Alloy Online, Inc., 17th Street Productions, Netmarket Group Inc., and Skytel and their respective advertising, promotion, production agencies and the affiliated companies of each are not eligible. Participation in this Sweepstakes constitutes contestant's full and unconditional agreement to and acceptance of the Official Sweepstakes Rules.

HOW TO ENTER: No purchase necessary. To enter, visit the Alloy Web site at www.alloy.com and answer each of the Fearless trivia questions on the entry form at the site. Submit your entry by fully completing the entry form. To be eligible for the grand prize you must answer each question correctly. Eligible entries will be entered into a random drawing for the grand prize. Chances of winning the grand prize depend on the number of eligible entries received. Entries must be received by September 30, 2000, 11:59 p.m., Eastern Standard Time. There is no charge or cost to register. No mechanically reproduced entries accepted. One entry per e-mail address. Simon & Schuster, Inc., Alloy Online, Inc., Netmarket Group Inc. and Skytel and their respective agents are not responsible for incomplete, lost, late, damaged, illegible or misdirected e-mail or for technical, hardware or software failures of any kind, lost or unavailable network connections, or failed, incomplete garbled or delayed computer transmissions which may limit a user's ability to participate in the Sweepstakes or any condition caused by events beyond their control which may cause this Sweepstakes to be disrupted or corrupted. All notifications in the Sweepstakes will be sent by e-mail. Sponsor is not responsible, and may disqualify you if your e-mail address does not work or if it is changed without prior notice to us via e-mail at contest@alloymail.com. Sponsor reserves the right to cancel or modify the Sweepstakes if fraud or technical failures destroy the integrity of the Sweepstakes as determined by Sponsor, in its sole discretion. If the Sweepstakes is so canceled, announced winner will receive prize to which s/he is entitled as of the date of cancellation.

RANDOM DRAWING: Prize Winner will be selected in a random drawing from among all eligible entries on October 1, 2000 to be conducted by Alloy Online designated judges, whose decisions are final. Winner will be notified by e-mail on or about October 3, 2000. Odds of winning the prize depends on the number of eligible entries received.

FEARLESS™

3011-01 (3 of 3)